SHADOWS

M J ROWLEY

SilverWood

Published in 2013 by the author
using SilverWood Books Empowered Publishing ®

SilverWood Books
30 Queen Charlotte Street, Bristol, BS1 4HJ
www.silverwoodbooks.co.uk

ISBN 978-1-78132-112-6

British Library Cataloguing in Publication Data
A CIP catalogue record for this book is available from the British Library

Set in Sabon by SilverWood Books
Printed on responsibly sourced paper

SHADOWS

Chapter 1

The strange thing was, the first time I thought I was about to die, I just seemed to relax. During this fraction of a second, time seemed to stop, as if to give me the chance to scan through the thirty-six years, eleven months and twenty-three days I had existed on this planet. It seemed my life had simply been an adventure, an adventure with unending complexities and contradictions I'd never given much thought to – until now.

If this was the end, well then this was it. I'd had some good times, got myself into a load of scrapes and had tried my hand at more things than I should have done – certainly more than most people twice my age had even thought of going for.

The car travelling towards me at some sixty to seventy miles an hour swerved into Rue du Faubourg Saint-Honoré, it mounted the pavement, then scraped along a garden wall before colliding with a refuse bin. The shower of garbage, airborne like a snow blizzard, made it obvious the bin was yet to be emptied by the local refuse service.

As if deciding I had too much to achieve, too many challenges I was anxious to grapple with, my sense of survival came to the fore. I would need, at the very least, another thirty-six years, eleven months and twenty-three days to achieve all the goals I'd set myself. In any case I was certainly not ready to depart from this mortal coil without a fight. My muscles tensed as I lurched back against the railings bordering the offices of Sotheby's International Auction House – allowing the oncoming car to pass and miss me by what must have been a mere couple of centimetres. I felt the wind hit my face and a sharp pain in my right arm as the wing mirror of this missile caught my elbow. The folder of papers I was holding scattered a few yards along the pavement and a black document case, thrown from the window of the car, landed among them.

Picking myself up I felt enormous relief, quickly followed by a cold shivering sensation I assumed to be the symptoms of shock. A further screech of brakes, this time accompanied by the sound of a police siren, made my muscles react as I again prepared to vacate the pavement. However, it quickly became apparent that the driver of this vehicle was either a more accomplished driver, or simply had a higher regard for the life of Parisian pedestrians. The driver, managing to keep all four wheels of his vehicle on the road, swept past.

A couple opposite, who had witnessed my narrow escape, came running over to me, since my understanding of French was zero, I assumed they were enquiring if I was alright and if I needed any help. I tried to assure them I was fine but it quickly became apparent that their understanding of English was on a par with my understanding of French. However, with many thumbs up signs and repetitions of "I'm okay", they eventually understood. I thanked them for their concern, picked up my papers together with the attaché case which had been thrown from the car, and continued the walk back to my hotel, the Hotel Campanile, about a quarter of a mile further along Rue du Faubourg Saint-Martin.

I was on my way back to the hotel after attending a last-minute appointment at the headquarters of Les Machines, arranged the evening before. This was my fourth day in Paris and my fourth visit to the company. I had been negotiating a contract with the transport director, Simon Chandler, in an effort to secure a contract for my company, MCL Carriers, to handle all deliveries of the machinery they manufactured for the construction industry. Some eighteen months ago they had purchased a medium-sized British engineering company, Northern Engineering. The company had been involved in manufacturing diggers, small cranes and drilling equipment for some twenty odd years or more for the construction industry. They'd never made much of an impression on the big concerns, JCB and Caterpillar – until, that is, a couple of years ago when the founder of the company, one George Whitecroft, designed and launched a new machine for underpinning properties suffering from subsidence. The idea was simple, and like most simple ideas the new system was proving to be a runaway success. A drilling mechanism together with a high pressure injection system was designed to bore holes under buildings requiring stabilising. Then a highly patented foam substance was pumped into the ground. This substance, when set, was every bit as strong and solid as the traditional mix of concrete and stone. The system eliminated the old drawn-out process of having to dig two metre diameter holes around the property then filling these with a mixture of concrete and stone. The new process enabled underpinning work to be completed in a quarter of the normal time and at well under half the cost.

When the process proved acceptable for laying foundations for certain types of new constructions, Les Machines made an offer to purchase Northern Engineering outright, making George Whitecroft an extremely wealthy man. The new owners took over production of the equipment at the factory in England and at a new factory they'd built next to their existing premises at Nantes, France.

The highly patented foam substance was to be distributed by a network of franchised suppliers across Europe and beyond. My task was to arrange transportation of the machinery to customers both in the UK and Europe.

My meeting had been a success. I had agreed some last-minute details and made the finishing touches to the contract I'd secured with their transport director. The contract was to handle all deliveries for the next twelve months and was big. This was going to be the start of my expansion programme – a programme designed to take my company from a six truck business turning over a mere £600,000 per annum to the big time. The contract I had managed to secure was worth in excess of £2 million per annum, minimum – and there was the chance of double that once I'd proved our service and reliability.

I felt an assortment of emotions running through me as I made my way back to the hotel. Excited by the contract I'd been successful in securing, grateful to be alive after my near-death experience a few moments earlier and anxious to convey the news of my success here in Paris to my girlfriend Carol and my secretary and personal assistant, Theresa. My transport business, MCL Carriers, had done quite well over the few years since I'd started the company but I was ambitious. I wanted to expand. I knew there was business out there. I was confident we could handle the expansion I'd planned, give an excellent service and make a decent profit.

As I arrived back at my hotel the few remaining clouds had disappeared and I felt the warm May sunshine on my face. This was my first visit to the capital but I wasn't altogether impressed. Nothing to do with the near-death experience a few moments earlier, but rather more to do with not understanding the language, and certainly not taking to the food. Anything other than sausage, egg and chips; steak, egg and chips or a curry on a Friday night was alien to me. The meals I'd been served during my four days here were not to my liking. How much of this was down to my inability to decipher the menus or grasp the waitress's interpretation of what was on offer I'm not sure, but the results were not good for me. I also thought the wine was a very poor substitute for the lager served at my local, the Crown Inn. I had already decided one of the first things I was going to do on my return home would be to down at least a couple or more pints of their special brew.

When our contract begins, my personal assistant (who assured me she was fluent in French) will certainly have her work cut out. Theresa had been with me since day one and was worth her weight in gold. I'd decided if my visit here in Paris was successful and I'd secured the contract with Les Machines then I would offer her a partnership in the business. This, together with the rest of the plans I'd been working on, I was *now* anxious to get under way.

Chapter 2

The reception area of the Hotel Campanile, while slightly dated, was nevertheless very impressive. The almost white, highly-polished marble floor tiles made a dramatic contrast with the black leather settees and armchairs. The walls, adorned with several gilt-framed prints of famous, or maybe not so famous, artists, all reflected their multitude of colours in the marble flooring, aided by an explosion of light from six enormous gold and silver crystal chandeliers. An impressive entrance, I thought, designed no doubt to give a feel of opulence and luxury to guests as they arrived, and probably to soften the blow when being handed the final bill upon leaving.

All of this, for me anyway, came a very poor second to the charms of Claudine Dupont, the hotel receptionist. She was a tall lady in her late twenties or early thirties, with long blonde hair and a slim, almost skeletal figure. She had the most beautiful green eyes, which seemed to pierce deep into my senses and almost tempted me to pursue her very beautiful and somewhat obvious smiles of invitation. Despite the temptation, I was behaving myself. I knew my girlfriend Carol, back in England, was the one for me. For the first time in many years, perhaps if I'm honest, the first time ever, I was behaving myself.

Walking up to the reception area, Claudine gave me one of her warm smiles as she handed me the keys to my room.

"Hello, Michael, what have you been up to this morning? You look like you've been dragged through a hedge backwards, and your jacket, the sleeve is all torn."

Not wanting to elaborate on the morning's events, I smiled.

"Oh that, I just slipped on the pavement a few moments ago. Good job I've got a change of clothes with me."

"You're leaving us today?"

"Yes, just off to my room to collect my things."

"Well, I hope you've enjoyed your stay and will come back again soon."

I assured Claudine that on my next visit to Paris I would stay at the Hotel Campanile. Apart from all the obvious attractions, she was the only person I'd met in France who had been able to communicate with me in an interpretation of the English language I could understand.

I walked across the reception area and took the elevator to the second floor. I opened the door to my room, threw my papers and the attaché case onto the bed, got showered, and changed into my jeans, a clean shirt and a jacket. My suit had had it. A large gaping hole in the sleeve and a tear in the trousers, plus some blood stains, confirmed I'd need to buy another when I got home.

"Marks & Spencer again," I said to myself. "I might go mad and get two."

With the plans I'd got for my business I'd probably need them. I opened the door of the fridge and took out one of the miniature bottles of whisky. It was only 11.15am but after the morning's excitement I thought, I've earned it.

Pouring the whisky into a glass I added two lumps of ice, took a swig, then picked up the phone to call Carol.

We'd been seeing each other for over eighteen months now. The attraction between us had been instant and I thought it was probably pointing towards the end of my bachelor days.

Carol had inherited her father's transport company and the

11

family home last year and was worth several million. This side issue played no part in my attraction to her. On the contrary, I found the situation embarrassing at times. I was determined rather than to feel in any way demoralised, I would work to bring my enterprise up to at least a million in value over the next couple of years or so. Then if things were still going strong, maybe then, we'd get ourselves well and truly hooked.

"Carol, I've got the contract and I'm on my way home."

"Michael, that's brilliant – so you can afford to take me out somewhere special this evening then? That's if you're not too worn out chasing all those Parisian girls."

"Carol I've been as good as gold over here and believe me I can't wait to get back home. We'll celebrate when I get back, anywhere you like. And by the way, I've decided to continue with the purchase of Birchwood House Farm. I'm going to telephone the agents and my solicitor in the morning and agree to the completion date they've pencilled in for next week. We can chat over the ideas I have this evening. It'll mean a hell of a lot of work for the next twelve months or so but I just know it's the way forward."

"I'm with you all the way, Michael, you know that, and don't forget what I suggested. If you need any help, you know... Well, anyway, it's always there, you know that."

"I do, Carol, and thanks. I'll be back this evening. My flight leaves at 3.55 this afternoon and we're due to land in Birmingham sometime after 5pm so I should be with you around teatime."

"Have a good journey, Michael. See you later."

One more call to make I thought, Theresa, then I really must check out. My receptionist friend Claudine had allowed me to keep my room for one extra night due to the last-minute appointment this morning, without adding this extra night's stopover to my account. The new guest, I was told, would be arriving around midday so I needed to get a move on.

"Theresa, it's Michael."

"Michael, how are you enjoying Paris?"

"I'm not. The food's rubbish, the wine's awful, I can't understand a bloody word anyone is saying and apart from all that, the traffic here, believe me it's lethal. But, the good news is, we have the contract."

"I knew you'd do it, Michael. Congratulations."

"A lot more work for everyone, Theresa. I hope you're up to it."

"No problem – when do we start?"

"August is when the first part of the contract begins so we've got to get a move on. I've decided to complete on Birchwood House Farm next week as planned, so we need to begin organising moving the offices there. So get that list ready you've been making of everything we need to do. I know the barns at Birchwood House Farm will make a perfect garage for servicing the trucks and Martin Cooper confirmed with me before my trip over here that there would be no objections for planning consent to use the paddock as a parking area for the trucks."

"When are you back home?"

"Coming back this afternoon. I'll be in the office in the morning. We'll close an hour earlier tomorrow, Theresa. I want to talk over some ideas I have so we'll get ourselves a drink or two at the Crown."

"I'll look forward to that. Have a safe journey."

I put down the phone and threw my ruined suit into the suitcase along with all my other gear, including my toiletries and spare pair of shoes. I gathered up all my papers from the bed including something I hadn't noticed – a letter which had slipped out of the attaché case (the one thrown from the car which had nearly ploughed me into the pavement just half an hour earlier.) I noticed much later that the envelope was handwritten and marked: 'For the personal attention of Martin Cartwright,' and in the top right-hand corner: 'To be collected.'

13

The letter was addressed to:
The British Embassy
35 Rue du Faubourg Saint-Honore
75363
Paris
CEDEX 08

Chapter 3

Guillaume Balaille and Matthieu Pierron had been in and out of
trouble since their early teens. Brought up in one of the poorer
suburbs of Paris, Guillaume and Matthieu had been partners in
petty crime for several years and had appeared in front of the local
magistrates no less than three times over the past couple of years.
At their last appearance, a few weeks previously, they were warned
that should they appear before the court again then a custodial
sentence would be handed down to them without hesitation. This
was their very last warning. The warning, however, seemed to make
only one difference: a determination simply to make sure next time,
they didn't get caught.

Stephen Davis, a junior clerk employed at the British Embassy
in Paris, was driving back to the embassy with a letter he'd been
instructed to collect from an antique dealer situated a short
distance away at Porte Saint-Denis. Unaware of how important the
contents of the letter were, Stephen stopped off at local newsagent
to buy some cigarettes. As he came out of the shop, to his horror,
he realised his utter stupidity. The car he'd been using had been
stolen.

Guillaume and Matthieu had been searching for over an hour
before the gift of a top of the range Mercedes, with coat and
attaché case clearly displayed on the rear seat, presented itself like

a gift from heaven. Thanks to practice and expertise, breaking the driver's window and making the required connections to the wires beneath the dashboard took just a few seconds. Like mechanics working for Ferrari in the pits at Monza, they completed their operation with an accomplished air of sophistication and professionalism. With a screech of rubber burning the tarmac, which would have impressed even Michael Schumacher, they drove off with their prize. Guillaume was the driver, leaving Matthieu free to go through the glove compartments, the pockets of the coat left on the back seat and the attaché case. Matthieu then began throwing everything considered of no monetary value out of the car window.

Stephen Davis's call to the embassy reporting the incident created a response bordering on panic when the British Ambassador made it clear to the French police the importance of recovering the documents which were in the car.

His call resulted in all police cars being alerted to the incident. Cars at Champs-Élysées, Rue de la Roquette and Porte Saint-Denis were radioed with instructions to drive towards Rue du Faubourg Saint-Honoré, hoping to create a net and corner the stolen Mercedes.

It worked. After a very short time our scoundrels, realising they had been well and truly cornered, pulled off Rue du Faubourg into one of the side roads. Not wishing to experience the custodial sentence promised at their last visit to the local magistrates court, they leapt from the car and made a successful getaway on foot. The car was quickly impounded by the French police followed by an immediate search for the attaché case, which according to the British Ambassador, contained items of national importance. The sometimes rather fragile diplomatic relationship with our Parisian neighbours took a slight turn for the worse that morning – at least with the Parisian police, as all leave was promptly cancelled until the return of the attaché case had been secured.

After an uncomfortable thirty-minute taxi ride consisting of sharp breaking, fierce accelerating and an excitable array of colourful language shouted by my driver at any vehicle daring to look as if it may come near to our cab, we eventually arrived at Charles de Gaulle airport. I checked in for my flight back to Birmingham. The airport was crowded and my difficulty in understanding anyone with the slightest accent made every question and answer routine twice as long to get through. The espresso coffee I ordered turned out to be a cappuccino with froth and a sprinkling of chocolate. Even with my half-Brummie, half-Irish accent, I could not understand how the word espresso could possibly have been mistaken for cappuccino. I decided not to delve further into this very obvious mistake made by the young lad serving at the coffee shop and walked out onto the balcony overlooking the runway.

I lit a cigarette and drank the coffee, which as it turned out, wasn't that bad. Despite all the distractions of the morning, my mind remained focused on my plans to go ahead with the purchase of Birchwood House Farm and complete the transaction pencilled in for next week. The plan was to move the offices there and use the surrounding three acres of grounds for housing some of the trucks. The barn would also make an ideal garage for servicing the trucks *vehicles.* I had agreed the price of £795,000 to purchase the freehold. After selling my apartment and paying off the mortgage, I had £265,000. This, together with the sale of my classic Jaguar XK150 (which I have to admit was the most difficult decision for me to make), gave me a further £65,000; this made up the total deposit I required of £330,000. I would be taking on a mortgage of £465,000, together with a bank loan of £50,000 to go towards the cost of getting the alterations underway which would be needed at the property. So far, I thought, just over half a million of liability. What the hell, I'll make all this work. In any case, I'll need to increase the business overdraft facility to at least £100,000 to finance the contract with

Les Machines. So, no time for cold feet. The boarding call for my flight came over the public address system, and I made my way down through the gangway and over to the aircraft.

The new guest at Hotel Campanile, Phillip Mason, found an attaché case in his room which he assumed to have been left by the previous occupant and returned it to the reception desk. The manager, noticing that the contents were the property of the British Embassy, immediately telephoned the police to report what had been found. Within minutes two police cars arrived and both the manager and Phillip Mason were questioned at some length by an Inspector Mainard. Eventually the inspector and his constables left the hotel, taking with them the attaché case for which they had strict instructions to return immediately to the British Embassy.

My flight landed on time at Birmingham Airport at 4.10pm. It was raining. I don't know why but every time I go away, whether it's a holiday or business trip, it always seems to be raining in Birmingham when I get back. Oh well, I thought, at least I can understand what everyone is saying, even if I don't want to hear it.

I consoled myself with the thought that a decent drink would not be far away. I went to the car park and got into the second-hand, somewhat battered Peugeot 307 I'd purchased a couple of weeks previously to take over from my beloved Jaguar XK150. I drove to Carol's house, The Beeches, Lapworth. Within ten minutes we were in bed together and apart from the occasional visit to the bathroom and the wine rack in the kitchen, remained there till 8am the following morning.

Chapter 4

Andrew Tallett had been parked in the car park at the rear of the Hotel Campanile for just over an hour. It was now 7.15am. His operation would commence in exactly five minutes, when he would walk through to the reception area, display his warrant card and ask the manager to page Phillip Mason.

Andrew Tallett had never thought of himself as an assassin. A defender of democracy, a guardian of the peace, but not really an assassin.

The information contained in the letter addressed to Martin Cartwright at the British Embassy in Paris could quite easily, in the wrong hands, pose a threat to the national security not only of the United Kingdom but the United States of America as well. Should the information ever reach the public domain, the shock waves would cause unimaginable problems. That threat therefore must be eliminated.

Tallett was simply responding to what he believed to be his patriotic duty. Conventional morality, as such, had no part to play. He concerned himself only with the broader picture. His assignments were usually politically motivated and nearly always, as he saw it, for the defence of democracy.

Tallett had been trained both by the CIA and the FBI. After retiring in 1998, he'd started a small but highly sophisticated security company with its base in Washington and an office in London.

The telephone call Tallett had received yesterday evening from one of his contacts in London outlined the events leading up to the loss of the letter addressed to the British Embassy and details of its contents. Taking a swig from a bottle of mineral water, Tallett put the warrant card he'd brought with him – in the name of Inspector Cearn of the French police department – into his inside jacket pocket. Then, after checking a small plastic capsule adhered to the underside of the middle finger of his left hand, he exited the car and walked across the car park into the reception area of the Hotel Campanile.

Walking up to the reception desk, he showed the warrant card and asked for Phillip Mason to be paged and meet him in the reception area. Ordering a pot of coffee for two, Tallett sat at one of the large settees at the far end of the hall next to the elevators.

The waitress brought over the coffee Tallett had requested just as Phillip Mason was exiting the elevator.

"Mr Mason, my name is Inspector Cearn. Sorry to bother you again, sir, but I need to go over a couple of things with you."

Phillip Mason was annoyed but he sat down on the slippery leather sofa.

"Okay Inspector but I really don't know how I can help you. I told what little bit I knew to your people yesterday."

"Just routine, sir," Tallett replied as he poured the coffee. "Please join me. I'll be out of your way in five minutes."

Tallett poured two coffees, and with a sleight of hand even the great illusionist Houdini would have envied, poured the liquid from the capsule under his finger into Mason's cup. The odourless liquid contained sodium fluoroacetate.

Phillip Mason was annoyed at having to explain, yet again, the very simple fact that he returned an attaché case he found in his room to the receptionist. He looked at Inspector Cearn, thinking come on then, ask your questions about that bloody attaché case and let's get out of here.

"Right, sir," continued Tallett, opening up a notebook. "In your statement yesterday you confirmed that after arriving at Charles de Gaulle airport at 6.15am you made your way over to the hotel here and checked in at 2pm. Is that correct?"

"Yes, that's correct."

"Then when you went to your room you found on the bed an attaché case which you handed to the hotel manager."

"Correct again, and that Inspector, is all I know."

"There's just one thing I need clarification on, sir. The airport is about forty minutes' drive from here so can you confirm where you were in the eight hours or so since arriving at Charles de Gaulle airport and your arrival here, at the Hotel Campanile?"

"Yes, I had breakfast with my nephew who's also over here on business. He knows Paris like the back of his hand and offered to spend the morning driving me around, showing me some of the sights before dropping me off here."

"And your nephew can confirm all this I take it."

"Yes."

Taking out a card from his wallet, Phillip Mason then handed it to Tallett.

"Here's his office address and telephone number. You can check all of what I've just told you with him whenever you like."

"Thank you, sir. And there's absolutely nothing else you remember about yesterday?"

"Absolutely nothing at all Inspector."

"Well, I think that's it for now. We've finished our coffees so I'll get out of your way. Thank you for your assistance."

Tallett walked out of the hotel, back to his car and drove off.

Phillip Mason was found dead on the floor of his room later that morning by one of the cleaners.

Chapter 5

The office was manic that afternoon. The telephones seemed busier than ever – more new business from our regular customers and the usual sprinkling of complaints and moans and groans from the drivers. In addition to all this, two of our trucks had broken down. Gordon, our mechanic, had driven over to the M6 just outside Wolverhampton to try to resolve the problem there – either to make good the repairs needed to enable the vehicle to reach its destination, or failing that, back to the garage for whatever repairs were required. The driver of the second truck had reported problems with the steering, which I guessed could have been caused by the hydraulic suspension playing up. His description of the problem – "It looks totally fucked to me, Guv" – was perhaps not the most helpful of reports. Eventually I managed to persuade one of the mechanics at Crossways Service Station on the Coventry Road, who we'd dealt with before, to go over to see if he was able to solve the problem.

In addition to the day-to-day running of MCL Carriers, Theresa and I were busy attempting to make lists of what would be required: firstly, with moving the offices to Birchwood House Farm next week and secondly, drafting a reorganisation programme to meet the increase in business from our contract with Les Machines, which was due to start in just over two months' time. I'd made an appointment with the business manager at Barclays Bank for the following afternoon to commence the process of begging for the first £50,000 increase to the company overdraft, which we were going to need. Everything felt heavy but I was prepared for it. I knew all that I'd planned was not going to be easy but my business sense told me profits were there to be made from the new contract I'd secured and that even without any further increase in business, it would be more than enough to hold the whole thing together. I was confident, but also aware the road ahead was going to be anything but easy.

Taking the contract I'd signed with Les Machines out of my briefcase, I noticed on top of the papers, a letter addressed to the British Embassy and marked 'To be collected.' It didn't take me long to realise this must have dropped out of the attaché case when I was collecting all the papers off my bed at the hotel. I put the letter in the top drawer of my desk thinking I'd post it on to the embassy in the morning.

"Come on, Theresa, let me get that drink I promised. I said we'd close an hour earlier today and it's already gone six o'clock. So come on, I've got something I want to chat over with you."

The rain that had been falling constantly that day had retreated to a light drizzle. We walked the few hundred yards or so from the office over to the Crown Inn. It was packed. A dull, wet Thursday in May and it seemed everyone needed at least one drink to ease the boredom created by our typical British summer. I ordered our drinks and joined Theresa at the table she'd managed to claim from the two previous occupants, who'd just retreated to the smoking hut recently erected outside in the courtyard. I could have done with a cigarette myself but that would have to wait.

"Theresa, how would you like to be a partner in MCL Carriers?"

A look of astonishment was followed by a few seconds of silence.

"Well, I wasn't expecting this." Theresa, almost dropping the packet of cashew nuts she was struggling to open, looked at me with goggled eyes. "When you said you'd got something you wanted to chat over with me I imagined it to be about our computer system or the move to Birchwood House Farm. A partner, Michael, is this for real?"

"Theresa, you know, or should do by now, that I couldn't manage without you. I want you to be part of the success I'm determined our business will achieve. You'll have no financial responsibility to worry about. I'll take care of all that. But if we're going to take our small, rather modest business to where I believe we should, and certainly can be, then I want you to be well and truly on board."

"Well, the answer is yes, Michael, definitely. I love the work and I'm excited about the expansion you're working on. So yes, where do I sign?"

"You don't need to, you know me by now. I'll confirm things by letter and at the end of the year, when our new contract is up and running, maybe we'll get that car of yours updated."

"What about your car, Michael? You've just had to sell your pride and joy, the Jaguar."

"No problem. I'll buy it back in six months' time. Either that or I'll get another one."

"That's what I said to my husband the other day. Keep bringing the business in and I'll take care of all the paperwork. And while we're having this informal chat, can I mention something to you? Not about the business, about Carol. When are you going to be sensible and settle down properly with her? You're both obviously a perfect match for each other and besides all that, I've seen this gorgeous two-piece suit in Debenhams and a hat to die for so I just need the right excuse to indulge myself."

Typical of Theresa, I thought. Like all women, she loves matchmaking.

"I've promised myself to get our business into shape first, Theresa. Get it to where it should be, then, when we've done that, maybe I'll buy that suit for you."

Noticing the couple who'd just taken up the table opposite holding two large plates of steak and chips, I suddenly felt quite hungry.

"Do you fancy something to eat, Theresa? I'm going for the steak and chips they serve here."

"No, I've got to get back. Otherwise Bernard will be decimating the kitchen trying to conjure up something for himself. Besides, now I'm a partner I'll need to get in a bit earlier tomorrow. There are a few things I'd like to change. No need to look worried, Michael – I doubt you'll even notice."

"You have a good night, Theresa, and give my regards to Bernard. I hope your kitchen is still intact when you get back."

I went over to the bar and ordered another pint, plus steak and chips. Halfway through the meal and second pint, I noticed at the far end of the bar a very attractive woman – late thirties, possibly early forties. She was wearing knee-high boots, tight black jeans, a short jacket and a bright red scarf. Her features were what I would describe as positive, rather angular, which gave her a very definite look of sophistication. But perhaps the other, most striking feature was her deep blue eyes. I had the feeling she'd been watching me. Not wishful thinking, just a feeling I had. She looked familiar. I was sure I'd seen her somewhere, but just couldn't place her.

I finished my meal, drained the last of my pint and decided on an early night. Looking out of the window I noticed it had stopped raining and decided to walk back to my apartment, which was only a couple of miles away. I thought the walk would do me good. Besides, two pints of lager at the Crown Inn was the equivalent of three pints of the more average beer. I walked across the bar area to the rear entrance when Harry, busy serving at the bar, called out to me.

"Michael, a woman asked me to give you this."

He handed me an envelope.

"Which woman, Harry?"

25

"No idea, Michael – some woman who was at the bar earlier. Don't worry. Your secret's safe with me. She looked a bit of alright as well."

I took the envelope.

"Thanks Harry. See you tomorrow."

I walked out of the Crown Inn and began walking back to the apartment. As I strolled along I opened the envelope Harry had handed me and took out the handwritten note inside. This was certainly one letter which had me guessing. I read it through, then read it again; three times I read through it, but could make little sense of it.

Michael,
You don't know me, but I need to speak to you concerning your recent visit to Paris. I dislike having to contact you in this rather cloak and dagger manner but what I need to discuss with you is very important. Please meet me at the Emperor's Palace restaurant, High Street, Deritend. I will be there from 8.30pm this evening.
Catherine

Chapter 6

I looked at my watch. It was 7.45pm. I decided to risk driving and went back to the office car park, collected my battered Peugeot and drove back to my apartment. The Emperor's Palace, Deritend. I'd heard of the place although it was one of the very few Chinese restaurants in Birmingham I'd not visited. I made a coffee, lit a cigarette and checked out the address of the restaurant in my A-Z.

With the location fresh in my mind I drove over to Deritend and parked the other side of the high street, a few minutes walk from the restaurant. I noticed a few lads hanging around a couple of hundred yards further on and if I'd been in my beloved Jaguar, there would be no way I'd have left it there. But the Peugeot: I doubted they'd be interested in that and it wouldn't exactly break my heart if they were.

I walked across the high street and over to the entrance of the restaurant, eager to discover what on earth was behind the mysterious note Harry had handed me just an hour previously. And what, if anything, all this had to do with my visit to Paris.

Immediately upon entering the restaurant I was greeted by a very smartly dressed oriental gentleman wearing an evening suit and black tie, whom I assumed to be either the owner or the manager.

A smile I can only describe as being energetically displayed was immediately followed by a poor, somewhat broken attempt at English, which unlike our French neighbours, I could at least understand.

"Good evening, Mr McLoughlan. Your guest, she is ready here. Please, you follow me."

How this guy knew who I was I had no idea, but I was not about to start asking any questions. Not yet, anyway.

I followed him through the restaurant. There was a scattering of customers taking up no more than five or six of the forty or so tables. This was Thursday evening. I reckoned most of the business in these places was created in the early hours of Saturday and Sunday mornings when all the clubs and bars had closed and the many diehards, reluctant to bring their evening's entertainment to an end, would continue their night out here.

We walked to the end of the restaurant to two large swing doors. The surrounding wall was adorned with enormous pictures of dragons and scenes of sunsets over beaches with imaginary oriental palaces in the background. We passed through the doors which my guide politely held open for me. Then, opening a door on the left of the corridor we'd just entered, he turned, bowed and said: "Please you make much comfortable here. Your waiter, he come soon."

I walked into the room which was a small area designed, I assumed, for private functions. Six tables neatly laid with all the utensils required to enjoy the culinary delights of the chef, Ma Wong, who, according to the plaques I'd noticed on our way through here, had been the successful recipient of several awards for Best Chef in the Midlands and one, if my first glance was correct, Best Chef in the UK 2009. Sitting at a table at the far end of the room was the lady I'd seen at the Crown Inn. I walked over to her and held out my hand, which she shook firmly, accompanied by a broad, friendly, and businesslike smile.

"Thank you for coming, Michael. Sorry about all the cloak and dagger business earlier, I'll explain everything in a moment. Can I get you a drink?"

Not wishing to push my luck with the alcohol limit I settled for a tomato juice.

Our waiter took the order: a tomato juice for me and glass of red house wine for my mysterious guest who I was still trying to place. Then it came to me. It was her voice that triggered my memory: a very distinctive, somewhat husky tone which confirmed it. Newsnight or one of the news programmes, reporting – if my memory was correct – one of the battles raging in Afghanistan, and again when reporting a suicide bombing somewhere in Baghdad.

Our waiter returned with the drinks.

"Can we smoke in here, Catherine?"

"I'm not sure, Michael," came the reply, as she offered me one of her Silk Cut cigarettes.

"But we'll soon find out."

I was beginning to take a liking to this mysterious lady.

"Thank you, but I'll stick to one of these," I said, as I opened my pack of Marlboro.

We lit up and I took a swig from my glass of tomato juice, then leant back slightly in the chair. I was becoming more anxious to discover what on earth this meeting was all about and what this very attractive TV presenter, no less, wished to discuss with me about my visit to Paris. I decided to open the conversation.

"I've seen you before, Catherine. Unless I'm mistaken you've presented items for Newsnight, or one of the news channels."

"Yes, I work for the BBC as a war correspondent and recently have not only had the task of compiling the reports but presenting them as well from time to time."

She seemed to cut short any further explanations and continued in a very businesslike manner.

"Michael, I know you're keen to discover what this is all about so I won't keep you in suspense any longer. Firstly, what I need to talk to you about doesn't really concern your visit to Paris as such, but due to a totally bizarre series of events when you were over there, I'm afraid you've landed yourself in the middle of an investigation I've been working on for the past couple of years. That investigation has now developed into something which is far too sensitive to present on Newsnight or any other media outlet come to that, at least for now. Last Tuesday, you were in Paris when a car belonging to the British Embassy was stolen. The car was stolen when the driver, a junior employee at the British Embassy, made a stop when returning to the embassy with documents he'd been instructed to collect earlier that morning. You'll no doubt remember the car, Michael – it was the one which passed you on your way back to the hotel and almost ran you down. The joyriders were throwing out of the car window anything they regarded of no value, including an attaché case which landed on the pavement next to you. Now you apparently, quite innocently, picked up this case and took it back with you to your hotel." Catherine hesitated for a moment. "Now, before I carry on, tell me: did you find a letter in the case, a letter addressed to a Martin Cartwright at the British Embassy?"

"Yes, as a matter of fact I did. I didn't notice it until this afternoon when I was going through all the papers I'd brought back with me after my appointment with Les Machines. I assumed it had dropped out of the attaché case when I was collecting everything together before checking out of the hotel."

Catherine sat back in her chair.

"Thank God for that. I hoped something like that might have happened."

Catherine's look of relief lasted just a few seconds.

"But you do still have the letter?"

"Yes, I was going to post it on to the British Embassy tomorrow."

"Then don't, whatever you do."

Catherine paused again, almost as if deciding the best way to continue.

"I think it's only fair, Michael you understand exactly what's going on and how bloody sensitive the situation is."

Hesitating again as if searching for the right words – something I thought a bit strange for an experienced news presenter – Catherine took another swig from her glass of wine and continued.

"Michael, your completely innocent involvement in all this has, I'm afraid, put you in some danger. I need your help, not only to complete my investigation but hopefully to get you out of the rather precarious situation you're in."

"Well, I'm certainly for that, but how on earth am I in danger? Who from? What the hell is all this about?"

Catherine sat back in her chair and while taking another swig of wine, gave me a searching look, as if deciding how much she was prepared to tell me. Then sitting back up, she placed her empty glass on the table and continued.

"I'll explain everything, Michael, it's the only way. Firstly, I must tell you the guest who took over your room at the Hotel Campanile after you'd vacated has been killed because he was assumed to be the only person who could have seen the letter – the letter that fell from the attaché case and is now, you tell me, at your office. The confusion arose when you unofficially stayed over for an extra night at the hotel. You were supposed to have checked out of your hotel on Monday evening. However, the receptionist at the hotel arranged for you to stay on due to your last-minute appointment, and as a favour, didn't enter this extra night's stopover on your account. Everyone has assumed Phillip Mason was the guy who was almost run down by the stolen car racing down Rue du Faubourg Saint-Honoré and he was the one who picked up the attaché case and took it back to the hotel. They've made the mistake of assuming Phillip Mason must be the only one who'd had access to the letter. It didn't take me to long to realise the mistake they'd made. The problem is I doubt it's going to take them much longer to realise that mistake either."

"Who's everyone? What the hell is this all about?"

"'Everyone', as I've just referred to them, are an assortment of interested parties. British intelligence, the KGB, the CIA, and several rogue agents, for want of a better description, out to make what they can from the situation for themselves.

The letter you now have holds information all these people are desperate to get hold of. It gives access to information which is not only vital to our security services, but to the United States as well. Then to complicate things further, it's probably worth several million to an assortment of interested parties who would quite happily sell that information on to the highest bidder."

"What about the guy who stole the car in Paris, the maniac who nearly ploughed me into the pavement?"

"Just a couple of young tearaways, arrested later that same afternoon. They didn't even have the intelligence to realise the car they nicked belonged to the British Embassy. It didn't take long to rule them out."

"And what is the information in this bloody letter, Catherine, or is that something you're just going to keep me guessing about? You know tomorrow I'm signing contracts committing myself to loans and mortgages in excess of half a million pounds. That together with all the planning and work I'm going to be committed to over the next twelve months or so is more than enough for me to handle without having to worry about the contents of a letter some idiot threw at me from the window of a car he'd just nicked."

Catherine momentarily glanced around the room. I assumed for the possibility of securing another glass of wine. As there was no waiter in sight, she settled for a top-up from the jug of water on the table. After taking a sip she wiped her mouth on one of the paper napkins then looked searchingly at me.

"I don't blame you for the way you're feeling right now, but bear with me for a moment. When I said the story I had been working on – which has now developed into an investigation with

MI6 – was big, I meant just that. It is very big. Before the invasion of Iraq we had agents working there, as did the FBI. They were sending through reports, a few of which were reasonably accurate, many were not so accurate and some, to use a well worn phrase, were 'sexed up.' The main reason behind the rather imaginative alterations made to the information supplied had nothing to do with security or patriotic idealism of the agents involved. It had everything to do with the fact that both the American and British governments were desperate for any information to help back up their claim that Saddam had weapons of mass destruction and posed a very definite threat to world peace. Now to complicate things further, these rogue agents, shadows as they're sometimes referred to, will be more than keen to get their hands on the information contained in the letter you have."

"Excuse my ignorance, Catherine but what exactly are rogue agents?"

Catherine smiled. "Yes I'm aware I'm trying to cram an awful lot in here I apologise for that but unfortunately the situation doesn't exactly give either of us much time. At the end of the Cold War, Michael, a lot of agents with MI6 and other countries' security organisations became redundant. These rogue agents are everywhere and would jump at the chance to secure a comfortable retirement for themselves. Any information they could get hold of, true or otherwise, would be offered for sale or kept secret, depending on who the negotiations were being conducted with.

Now there was an agent working for MI6 in Iraq, code named Snowstorm, who contacted MI6 a couple of years ago, claiming to have photographs of ballistic missiles being manufactured at two factories in Iraq prior to the invasion. One of the factories was located at a farm just outside Baghdad, the other was some underground factory inside the capital. The photographs apparently clearly showed the production of ballistic missiles capable of carrying an assortment of warheads held by the Saddam regime pretty well anywhere in the Middle East and beyond. The biggest bombshell, so to speak, was the fact the photographs showed that the equipment and the drafts of the technology being used had been supplied to Saddam by this country and the United States. Now this agent, Snowstorm, had also come into possession of letters between our government and the head of Saddam's secret service confirming the story which had been encircling MI6 long before the invasion – that this technology and all the necessary machinery and supplies had been made available to Saddam and his cronies to assist Iraq to win the war with Iran. Had the plan worked, it would have solved a multitude of problems for the West, not least of all how to deal with Iran and their nuclear ambitions. It would have also given this country and the US influence over oil supplies of both those countries."

I was attempting to take in all Catherine was telling me and was struggling with the reality of what she was saying.

"And what about Iraq's nuclear programme? Did that exist too? Were we helping them with that as well?"

"No. Not to put too fine a point on it, that dishevelled lot were incapable of organising a piss up in a brewery, let alone the highly sophisticated procedure required for the development of nuclear warheads. However, according to the MI6 agent Snowstorm, the information which had come into his possession confirmed the Iraqis were literally a few weeks away from being capable of firing long-range ballistic missiles."

"Hence the urgency," I said, "to get into the country and destroy the evidence. I just can't believe this, it's like a bad fucking dream. And the weapon inspectors, did they know about all this?"

"More than likely. However, there is another theory: the theory the photographs and letters may have been faked."

"Well, doesn't anybody bloody know?"

"The simple answer to that, Michael is that if they do, they're not saying. Not at the moment anyway. I've learnt that the sum of £2 million for the photographs, the negatives and all the letters has been agreed with Snowstorm. £1 million, I'm told, has already been paid and a further million has been agreed on receipt of the documents."

"So this agent Snowstorm, or whatever his name is, has been paid £1 million without any proof that he has the originals and if he does, if they're actually genuine."

"What I've uncovered so far, Michael, is the government and security services of both this country and the United States will at the moment agree to almost anything to get hold of these documents, which tends to suggest that some of them, if not all of them, could well be genuine. However, it could be that even if all the documents are fakes the security services believe any story of this kind is best kept buried."

"So the letter from this agent Snowstorm, in the process of being delivered to the embassy in Paris when their car was stolen, gives the location of these documents. Having just escaped from being hammered into the pavement stones of Rue du Faubourg Saint-Honoré I'm now holding information every secret service agency in the world would be more than happy to kill for, not to mention all the rogue agents you've just described looking for a nice little earner for themselves. Well, Catherine, how about you come back with me to my office now, collect the letter, and just leave me well and truly out of all this."

Catherine looked at me, her sharp blue eyes burning into me as if attempting to assess if she'd already said too much, given away too many secrets.

"No, Michael, it's best we're not seen together. It's possible I'm being watched. So for your safety as well as mine, we need to handle things a little more carefully than that. We must do things in a certain way. Firstly, tomorrow make a copy of the letter, then post the original to this address. Don't make a special journey. Post it with the rest of your mail at the office, in the normal way."

Catherine passed me a piece of one of the paper napkins she'd written an address on, somewhere in London.

"Then just as a precaution, until the original is received, put the copy in a waterproof packet, plastic bag, that sort of thing, and bury it. When I say bury it, Michael I mean just that. Don't keep it either at your house or office. Take it to the local park somewhere and bury it, and make sure you're not seen.

Thirdly, and most importantly, don't under any circumstances reveal a word of this to anyone – and I do mean anyone. Not a word, Michael about our meeting this evening or anything I've just told you."

All that was simple enough but there was just one thing I needed to ask, one very obvious question I thought.

"Forgive me asking the obvious, Catherine but I don't know you. We've never met before. So tell me, how can I trust you? How do I know you're not actually one of those rogue agents you've just described to me?"

"You don't, Michael. I wasn't sure whether to reveal this but…. There is something else you've got to get your head around I'm afraid. I'm working on this investigation at the request of MI6 and unfortunately they don't supply identity cards or letters of reference so you're just going to have to trust me."

"Looks like I've got no choice."

Catherine looked thoughtful.

"When's your birthday, Michael?"

A funny question I thought.

"As it happens, next week: the 29th. Why?"

"Nothing, just a thought. Now if you need to contact me don't try any other way than telephoning this number. This is my partner George's mobile number. Meanwhile, if there's anything I need to update you about I'll get a message to you."

After what was the most mind-boggling evening I think I'd ever spent, I made my way back to the car. I was still trying to take in all Catherine had told me, and still trying to decide if it was all completely true. I had absolutely no way of knowing, and no real alternative I thought, but to follow through what she'd asked me to do.

It had stopped raining, and as if summer was trying to tell us it had not completely abandoned us, the air felt slightly warmer and the clouds had cleared. Maybe tomorrow will be better.

As I walked up to my car, I smiled to myself. At least something this evening was a little more down to earth. I was right about those lads – they'd had more sense than to even contemplate nicking my rather battered 307. It did have some benefits then I thought, as I started the somewhat tired and noisy engine to drive back to my apartment.

Chapter 7

The following morning was busy. After an early start at the office and checking over a quotation Theresa had prepared for an enquiry received last week I telephoned Crossways Garage. I needed to check the state of play with our truck which had broken down yesterday. Theresa, who also arrived early, was busy returning all the messages left on our answerphone.

After checking over the quotation for the new enquiries we'd received I took the opportunity of dealing with the letter. I'd resisted the temptation of collecting last night, after my meeting with Catherine at the Emperor's restaurant. Taking the envelope from the top drawer of my desk, I opened it and took out an A5 sheet which was type written and simply said:

MOUSE
SEW O
1 14 7 20 9

Absolutely nothing else – no signature and no confirmation of the sender, which didn't exactly surprise me. There were just two words: mouse, sew and the letter O or the number zero and seven numbers. I had somehow expected something like this, some sort of coded message, but this, this I thought could mean just about anything. I began to wonder if all this was for real as I put the letter under the office copier. I took one copy as instructed and placed the original in an envelope I'd typed out with the address Catherine had given me. The copy I put in my inside jacket pocket. I decided – as there were so many things I needed to get through today – the plastic bag and burying routine would have to wait. Theresa was going to be busy interviewing potential office personnel and Gordon had a similar task in his efforts to find a good and reliable junior mechanic to assist in the servicing and maintenance of our trucks. Our business was going to increase fourfold very soon. We needed to prepare and equip ourselves, and not only that, but move the whole operation to Birchwood House Farm next week. The office, the service area, and all the equipment. I had two appointments today: one with the business manager at Barclays Bank at 11am, the other with my solicitors at 2pm to sign contracts not only for the completion on the sale of my apartment next Tuesday but also the contracts for completion of my purchase of Birchwood House Farm on Wednesday.

I'd arranged to stay at Carol's Tuesday night. An arrangement I thought may well be extended for at least another week. I'd still not ordered any 'white goods' for the kitchen. The previous owners, after my battle to reduce their asking price by some £75,000, were definitely not leaving the Aga or the rather handsome American style fridge-freezer. I couldn't blame them. In any case, cooking anything on an Aga would be totally alien to me and I was certainly not interested in learning about anything more complicated than a microwave. Having dropped mine when clearing the kitchen cupboards before my trip to Paris I was aware of another of the tasks I had today – a visit to the local Argos store to purchase a replacement.

I made sure the letter I'd addressed, as per Catherine's instructions, was left in our post tray. As I left the office I waved to Theresa, who was still busy on the telephone returning all the calls left on the answerphone, and drove over to the town and the first of my appointments with Barclays Bank.

The appointment went well. My business manager, Michael Evans, confirmed head office had agreed that my overdraft facility could be increased by £50,000 (although with some restrictions) and this arrangement would start immediately once my purchase of Birchwood House Farm had completed. He also supplied me with the telephone numbers of three contacts he thought would be helpful. The first, a leasing company within the Barclays group who he assured me would be able to quote competitive rates for leasing the extra trucks we were going to need. A second contact he was keen to point me towards was a company called Commercial Transport Answers, who recently set up supplying second-hand refurbished trucks, for sale or rental. And the third contact, a company image creator.

"Perhaps, Michael, it's time to update your image."

I agreed with this suggestion as I attempted to hide the burn marks on my shirt collar I'd made with the iron this morning in my usual rush to get out.

"A company logo on all your stationery and maybe the trucks as well can earn you a lot of extra business. Advertising is a very powerful tool. Try and make time to chat things over with these people. Ask for John Russell. Tell him I've recommended him to you."

All very useful contacts and the loan I required secured and agreed, albeit with security against Birchwood House Farm. Not a bad morning's work so far, I thought.

I shook hands with the manager and went downstairs to the main reception area, walking over to the counter to pay in some cheques and cash. More often than not I was lucky enough to be served by Kirsty, whose smile, like all the girls at this branch of Barclays, had the potential to attract more customers than all the cut-price mortgage deals and loan offers put together. If there was one thing this great bank was certainly doing correctly it was their choice of personnel.

My paying in book was stamped, initialled and returned to me with another very warm smile from Kirsty. After leaving the bank I began to walk up the high street. I was trying to decide where to grab something to eat when I noticed a dark red Toyota hatchback parked a little way down from Marks & Spencer. Nothing unusual about this, I thought, except I had the feeling I'd seen this earlier in my rear view mirror, on my way over to the town. I made a note of the registration number but couldn't help feeling I was probably mistaken and being overly dramatic. These suspicions, not exactly of danger but more of the uncertainty about all Catherine had explained to me yesterday, were going through my mind. The wars, the acts of terrorism, the double dealings and rogue agents – the shadows as Catherine called them. Are we ever actually told the truth or is everything to do with national security just covered up? Her revelations last night had me thinking but I was busy. I'd got one hell of a lot on and assumed the events in Paris and all that Catherine had revealed to me would eventually be taken care of by our security services. In any case, I just hoped I'd be left well out of it from now on.

I grabbed a Cornish pasty from Greggs in the high street and ate it as I walked round to the main shopping square. I got an espresso coffee from the Costa coffee house and sat outside at one of their tables. I lit a cigarette and took the letter I'd copied earlier out of my inside jacket pocket, the letter which apparently gave the location of the original photos, negatives and letters, which from what Catherine said last night, MI6 and every other security organisation were keen to get hold of, not to mention the rogue agents she'd described to me. The sky was clear and the sun felt warm on my face. Perhaps summer was making a brief visit. I had an idea: a weekend in Bournemouth wouldn't go amiss.

As soon as I've finished the appointment with my solicitors, I thought, I'll telephone Carol – she'd love a weekend away. No talk of business, moving house, haulage contracts or indeed anything else, just a weekend of doing nothing, hopefully soaking up some sun, and a couple of days eating all the wrong things and drinking too much.

I opened the letter I'd kept in my jacket pocket, and stared at the typewritten note.

MOUSE

SEW O

1 14 7 20 9

What the hell did it mean? Mouse what? Mouse droppings... And Sew O, what did that mean? Sewing something, stitching... sewer... Had the location details been left in a sewer somewhere? After Catherine's suggestion I bury this copy of the letter in the local park I wouldn't be surprised what this coded message could mean. Perhaps the photos had in fact been buried in a sewer.

The only other thought I had was perhaps mouse was short for mousetrap. That possibility brought to mind the play by the famous author Agatha Christie. I'd read many of her books some years previously but hadn't seen the long-running play, although I had been promising myself one day I would. There was nothing in her stories I could remember which remotely related to the interpretation of a coded message. However, I wished I could talk all this over with Miss Marple. She'd soon have all the answers.

It was almost 2.30pm. Time for my appointment with Charles Dixon, the solicitor at Gainsborough & Partners who dealt with the company's conveyancing work. I'd met Charles when purchasing my apartment five years ago and wasn't looking forward to the meeting. To purchase a simple two-bedroom apartment took Charles over an hour, with his question and answer routine to get through the pre-contract enquiries. I suppose he has to somehow justify his company's charges but I wished he didn't try so hard. I'd been in business long enough to know that when someone needs specialist advice, the specialist will ensure he makes his money.

We all do it. It's all par for the course. I walked across the square and into their offices. It took two very long hours this time but as important as the sale and purchase of the properties were, I really thought things were being taken a bit too far when I was told that a charge of £25 was to be made for each electronic transfer of funds to and from the bank or building society, with my solicitor making a further charge for overseeing this very simple transaction. I didn't comment, I just smiled, signing several times where requested and felt like a prisoner being released on parole as I walked out from the offices and into the town square. I lit a cigarette and telephoned Carol.

"How do you fancy a weekend in Bournemouth?"

"Love to. When?"

"In about half an hour. We could be there in time for dinner."

"Best idea you've come up with since asking me out on our first date."

"Okay, I'll be at yours in about half an hour. I'll have to buy some clothes when we get there. I'm not going back to the apartment to start rummaging through the wash basket, or going through the cases I've packed."

Carol laughed.

"You're bloody hopeless, Michael. We can stop off on the way and get you kitted out with a few things. And don't take offence, but how about we take my Land Rover?"

I wasn't in the least offended. On the contrary, I was relieved. I was confident now that we had a reasonable chance of reaching Bournemouth.

"Good idea Carol."

"We could stay at the Cedar Lodge Hotel. My dad used the place a lot for our family holidays. It's not only very good, but if the same owners are still there then we'll get good service."

"Okay Carol, you reserve a room and I'll see you in about half an hour."

I telephoned Theresa, brought her up to date with my plan for a weekend in Bournemouth, confirmed all the contracts had been signed and said that I would look forward to seeing her on Monday, to start the week of the big move.

Chapter 8

After grabbing a few things to wear plus a bag of toiletries from the local Marks & Spencer store we set out for Bournemouth. The traffic was not heavy and we arrived at the Cedar Lodge Hotel at just turned 8.30pm.

The original owners, Mark and Kathy Travers, were still at the helm, and Carol was right, we were treated like long-lost friends. After a meal we retired for the night. Our room overlooked the seafront and was decorated and furnished to perfection. We went to bed and stayed there until the buzz of Carol's travel alarm woke us at just turned 8am. We had breakfast, and as the promised sunshine had actually materialised, we absconded to the beach. We went swimming and ate like pigs, eating everything from burgers to toffee apples and candy floss, together with more energy drinks than I can remember, all displaying the promise of turning you into a top-performing athlete. We spent a fortune on every gaming device housed both on the pier and in the amusement arcades adorning the seafront. In the evening we went to a show at the Winter Gardens and finished a perfect day at Hussain's Curry House, situated about a fifteen-minute walk from the hotel.

I say finished a perfect day, but not quite finished. I felt good about not needing another energy drink to complete our own private entertainment until the early hours back at our hotel suite.

Again the buzz of Carol's travel alarm at 8am woke us to another warm and sunny day. We spent most of the time walking or just lazing about on the seafront. The initial novelty of the amusement arcades had receded somewhat, apart from the fact that our attempts yesterday proved the chances of winning any of the prizes, ranging from a simple tube of Smarties up to the thousand pound jackpot, all described as being so easy to achieve, were in fact totally impossible to get near to.

So a little more like a sensible, respectable couple and less like teenagers just out of school, we enjoyed the sunshine, the sea air and just being together. I'd almost forgotten the encounter in Paris or the meeting with Catherine. I was instead just looking forward to the move to Birchwood House Farm where I could get to grips with all the challenges which lay ahead. The challenge to expand my business and meet the targets I'd set myself. Not least the possibility of making the girl at my side forever happy.

After tea at the hotel I settled our account and put our cases in the Land Rover ready for our journey back to the Midlands. As we were about to get into the car, I had an idea.

"Carol, let's take one last walk along the beach before driving back."

Hand in hand we walked along the sands.

"Come on Carol," I urged, taking off my shoes and socks. "I've not done this since I was a kid."

Holding Carol's hand we splashed into the sea, kicking the waves as they ran towards us.

"Let's get out of here before we step on one of those bloody jellyfish things."

"Jellyfish things, what exactly are jellyfish things?"

"Jellyfish Carol. I remember stepping on one when I was a kid and believe me they sting like bloody hell."

She laughed.

"Not very brave are you?"

"You wouldn't say that if you trod on one."

Grabbing Carol's hand, we ran back to the beach.

Laughing and joking we climbed into the Land Rover to begin the journey back home. The banter between us continued as I attempted to dry my feet with some paper napkins I'd pocketed from the hotel. The weekend had been very special and had taken me a million miles away from all the events of last week. So much so that I failed to notice a dark red Toyota hatchback parked just fifty metres or so from the entrance to our hotel.

Chapter 9

Mickey Whitehead, a tall, balding, unpleasant sort of character in his early seventies, had run his pornographic bookshop in Soho since the late 1960s. Just like every morning for the past forty-six years, including Sundays, he unlocked the front door of his establishment at just turned 10am. It was Monday, the start of another week for Mickey's Private Images.

With the aid of his penknife, Mickey opened the two parcels containing the latest magazines from his supplier in Amsterdam and briefly flicked through the pages of one of the compilations of pornographic works of art. He mumbled to himself, "Another load of crap – not a patch on my own work."

Mickey was in fact a very accomplished photographer and cinematographer. He'd converted the upstairs of the shop to house two studios for the production of his home-made photographs and blue movies. He turned out over a thousand images a year, featuring every conceivable pose achieved by the scores of would-be models and actresses who called at the premises in the hope of pursuing their ambitions in finding an opening for a career in acting or modelling. The photographs and at least a few dozen movies, from The Plumber Calls to his latest work of art, It Takes Three to Tango, could have made Mickey a very wealthy man had it not been for the hefty protection racket charges he was forced to pay out every Friday evening. That was something he'd done as far back as the days when the Kray twins were in charge. Nothing much had changed – just the names of those running the same system.

Mickey began displaying the latest editions along the twenty or so shelves which encircled his shop.

Around the corner, just off the Tottenham Court Road, a dark red Toyota hatchback pulled up. Two heavily-set guys wearing almost identical long black overcoats – so obviously out of place on what was promising to be another warm and sunny day – walked down the Tottenham Court Road and into one of the narrow side streets. Two women hoping for the opportunity of an early start to their business stood in the doorway of one of the not-yet-open strip clubs, The Fallen Angel, owned apparently by some gangster character known by the name of Johnny Black. There was speculation that he was a nephew of the Richardson brothers, the notorious gangsters who ruled London in the 1960s and had overshadowed the Kray twins, not only thanks to their expertise in making a fortune from their varied criminal activities, but by keeping the fortune and avoiding spending most of their life behind bars. Their less successful counterparts, the Krays, had not been so lucky – one spending in excess of thirty years in a cell 8' x 10' while the other was forced to while away the same number of years in a secure psychiatric institution. The Richardson brothers on the other hand, had enjoyed freedom and a luxurious lifestyle supported by the proceeds of their many criminal activities. However, things had changed over the years. It was no longer a competition about which gangster was the 'Mr Big', and no one person seemed to hold a monopoly anymore. A bit like privatisation, the competition rules had changed somewhat.

"Looking for a good time, mister?"

One of the two stocky guys looked across to the woman in the doorway posing the question.

"Starting a bit early aren't you?" he replied with a grin.

"I can be here anytime you like if you're interested."

The reply came quickly from a woman well practised in the art of retaining the attention of any male who looked affluent enough to meet the hourly rate charged for her expertise.

"A bit busy this morning, love."

The two guys continued walking to their destination, Mickey's Images.

Entering the shop, the second of the guys turned the sign on the door to 'Closed' and silently dropped the catch. Mickey, still busy arranging the new supply of magazines, turned around.

"Can I help you guys?"

"We're here to collect the packet – the one you're holding on behalf of Snowstorm, Mickey."

"I've still not been paid yet. Five hundred quid is what was agreed. Do you have the money?"

The guy standing nearest to Mickey had heard it all before. No £500 fee or any other amount had been agreed. Mickey was simply holding some papers he'd been asked to look after a couple of weeks earlier.

"You could get people into trouble saying things like that, Mickey, making us think one of us had pocketed your fees. Not good you know, to start creating those sort of suspicions."

Taking a Beretta M9 with silencer out of his pocket, he pushed down the safety catch as he looked Mickey in the eyes.

"Tell you what, Mickey, you hand over the packet and we'll forget all about your indiscretion."

Mickey had dealt with gangsters from all levels of the underworld over the years, including ones used from time to time by the security services. He instinctively knew these gentlemen were not ones to push any further.

"Okay, can't blame a guy for trying."

Mickey went behind the counter, dialled the combination into the door of the safe underneath and took out an A4 sized, sealed

50

envelope and handed this over to the guy holding the Beretta M9.

"That's better, Mickey. Now you'd better lock the safe before someone is tempted to help themselves to whatever else you've got hidden away in there. Mickey stooped down and closed the door to the safe, then spun the combination lock. Immediately two bullets fired almost silently from the Beretta and went through the back of Mickey's head. The two guys left the shop and drove to Heathrow airport to catch their flight to Germany.

Another meeting was about to take place in the capital that morning, just a short distance away in Westminster.

Jacqueline Myers, the Home Secretary, had left Downing Street five minutes earlier on her way to MI6 Headquarters for her pre-arranged meeting with Sir David Gough, head of the Secret Intelligence Service.

At the Prime Minister's request, she had been given the task of overseeing the operation code named Aries and was to keep him personally informed of all progress – on a daily basis if necessary.

Myers, a rather plump forty-two-year-old, had bulldozed her way from MP for Redditch, West Midlands, and into the cabinet office. She was handed the job of Home Secretary after the Prime Minister's reshuffling procedure, which followed the resignation of Paul Barton, MP for Kenilworth and Minister for Transport – a hasty departure designed to defuse the backlash caused by revelations concerning the aforementioned's expenses irregularities, which were uncovered by one of the national newspapers.

She was well known for her short temper and bullish approach to even the simplest of situations. This unpleasant side to her character was matched only by her ability and expertise to switch, portraying the most charming, cordial and hard-working of public servants at the very second any one of the many interviews she gave commenced. This ability, which seemed to be improving by the day due to the forthcoming general election in a few months'

time, would be envied by the most talented of character actors.

Sir David Gough's private office was situated on the third floor of MI6 headquarters. Sir David was a very resourceful man, clear thinking and unflappable. Any idealism he may have held in the early years of his service at MI6 had evaporated long ago in more than one of the many operations he'd undertaken in a number of the far-flung outposts of the former British Empire.

The door to his office burst open and before Sir David's secretary could announce the arrival of the Home Secretary, Jacqueline Myers stormed into the office, closely followed by her undersecretary and bodyguard. Myers sat opposite Sir David and slapped a folder down on his desk, which she then opened.

"Right, I've no time for bullshit – are we any closer to getting hold of those bloody photographs or not?"

"Our agent, Home Secretary, is very close to achieving just that. Had it not been for a rather unfortunate incident in Paris the other day we'd have them by now, safely locked away."

"The fact is, Sir David, we don't. I've read your rather embroidered report detailing the loss of some attaché case on its way to our embassy but I can't help wondering why your agent didn't act quickly enough to avoid yet another total cock-up. Firstly, you tell me some junior clerk at the embassy in Paris loses the information when stopping off to buy cigarettes. You then go on to elaborate on your agent's report of this event but fail to explain why the hell she did nothing."

"On the contrary, Home Secretary, she handled the situation extremely well. We now have, I understand, the location of all the photographs including the negatives and the letters our agent Snowstorm discovered in Iraq. I would also add, Home Secretary, we do not have responsibility for the employment of the personnel at our embassy in Paris."

"No, but you do have responsibility for your own agents. I don't need to remind you Sir David, your man Snowstorm is probably only one of a number of rogues supposedly checked out by your organisation before being given full status."

"Point taken, but just in case of any further complications in this matter, I have, as a precaution you understand, made some enquiries as to whether it would be possible to produce negatives from the copies we hold to suggest the photographs are in fact fake. This would only be a precautionary measure but it just may be the answer to any further blackmail attempts, whether from the KGB or any rogue agent who may take an interest. But before I ask for this possibility to be investigated further, may I ask you Home Secretary, are the photographs fake, or are they in fact genuine?"

Jacqueline Myers stared eyeball-to-eyeball with Sir David Gough. Her face like thunder, the suggestion of a twitch in her right cheek made her remove her glasses as an excuse to scratch the irritating area. The few seconds seemed like hours.

Sir David relaxed slightly, then sitting back in his chair, and with the look of an experienced advocate who'd just succeeded in putting the vital question to secure the fate of the accused, continued: "You don't know, do you? The Prime Minister hasn't told you, has he?"

With an explosion of venom, Myers slammed shut the folder in front of her. She stood up and turned towards the door.

"Just keep me informed immediately of any progress you may possibly manage to achieve here. Immediately please, Sir David."

Her undersecretary and bodyguard – both quite used to this sort of occurrence – nodded in acknowledgement to Sir David and calmly followed their boss from the office. The door slammed and Sir David, with a wry smile, mumbled to himself, "Well that's one question you've just answered for me."

The door knocked again and was followed by the entrance of Peter Astor, one of Sir David's colleagues and closest friends.

"She didn't stay long did she? Hope you weren't too rude to her."

"I'm never rude Peter, you know that."

"Anyway, how's this Aries business progressing, David? Any problems?"

"Nothing more than the usual. Our agent is close to things. I remain, Peter, as always, optimistic."

"Who've we got on this one?"

"Catherine McKenzie."

Peter looked thoughtful for a moment.

"The war correspondent from the BBC? Do you think she's the right choice? I think I'd have chosen one of our more experienced people."

"She's more than capable, Peter. I have every faith in her. Besides, we do have two of our operatives shadowing her every move."

"Well, I hope you're right. This one has all the makings of being something very nasty if it goes wrong." Peter hesitated for a moment. "However, I suppose on the plus side, if things do go wrong then we can deny all knowledge of the situation."

"Yes, Peter. Now, before you start telling me none of us would be here if it wasn't for 9/11 you'll have to forgive me, I've things I need to catch up with."

Peter made his way to the door.

"Will we see you at the club later?"

Sir David looked up from the desk.

"Is our chef back yet?"

"No, next Monday, I'm told."

With a look of some disappointment Sir David thought for a moment.

"Maybe just a drink then, Peter, about eight o'clock."

"See you later then, David."

Chapter 10

The weekend in Bournemouth was one of the best ideas I'd had for a long time. I knew the next few days were going to be hard going and the couple of days' break had done me the world of good. It had allowed me to recharge my batteries, and recharged batteries were certainly something I was going to need.

I was right: Monday and Tuesday were as I'd expected, absolutely manic. I was at the office at just turned 7.30am on Monday and the phone was ringing before I'd had time to make a coffee and get to my desk. Three calls confirming new business and two calls from Crossways Service Station with quotations for the repairs needed for our truck that had failed to make it last Friday. Also, a call from Matt, one of the drivers who was unable to get in today, apparently due to a bout of influenza. Either that, I thought, or too much beer at the weekend. Then there was a complaint from one of our oldest customers over a delivery last week which had arrived on Wednesday and not Tuesday as promised. Then two more enquiries requesting written confirmation of charges quoted over the phone last week for collecting two small diggers from the manufacturers at Cannock and delivering them to the contractor's site just outside Edinburgh.

I was relieved, to say the least, when Theresa arrived at just turned 8am.

"Am I glad to see you. Bloody phone hasn't stopped and the answerphone's been flashing at me since 7.30am this morning. Just haven't had a minute to get to it so I know there's more on there to deal with."

"I'll make you a coffee first, Michael, then you can get on with all your paperwork."

It never ceased to amaze me how Theresa was able to cut herself off from any drama going on – something which seemed to be happening on a daily basis recently. She had the knack to simply attend to all the problems requiring attention in her usual calm and very matter of fact way – something I'd never been able to master. If there was more than one problem to be solved at any one time, everyone knew about it. I'd arranged for three of our drivers, Jim, Ray and Barry, to collect all the furniture from my apartment, excluding the fridge, freezer and washing machine which I'd agreed would be included in the sale. The trucks with all my gear would then be parked overnight in the garage at the rear of the depot, all ready for delivery on Wednesday to Birchwood House Farm. Carol had arranged for cleaners to go over the apartment as soon as Jim, Ray and Barry had humped out all my possessions. She'd also reminded me, on several occasions, to take note of all the meter readings. My solicitors had sent letters advising all the utility suppliers of the change of occupier. Telephone lines had been ordered for our new offices at Birchwood House which were faithfully promised to be up and running by Wednesday afternoon. Our main line at our existing depot would automatically transfer all calls to the new number for the next few months. Theresa had finished interviewing the applicants for the office personnel and had decided on two new members to join us next week. With her usual good planning, she had arranged for both of them to start this morning at 9am for a 'week's trial', as she'd described it to them. The result was that we were soon going to have the much needed extra help.

Gordon had been less successful with his efforts in finding a reliable mechanic to help with the servicing and repairs of our trucks so I decided to pay for the services of a recruitment agency specialising in this field. I made the decision to use the same agency to recruit the extra drivers we'd need in a couple of months' time.

I'd arranged for John Russell, the guy my business manager at Barclays had recommended, to call to discuss his ideas for updating our image and to design a logo for the trucks and our stationery. I'd already decided to let Theresa deal with that task. I also had an appointment with the second of my business manager's recommended contacts: the leasing specialist who would be able to give me quotations for leasing the extra trucks we'd need for the Les Machines contract. As soon as his quotation was with me I could then make all the necessary comparisons.

All in all, Monday was proceeding reasonably well. We'd received an early order from Les Machines to collect three of the underpinning systems from the Liverpool factory for delivery to one of their customers just outside Hamburg. The delivery was required for Tuesday or Wednesday next week. I confirmed this would present no problem. However, after checking the workload I realised I'd probably be making that delivery myself. No problem though. I'd made the trip many times over the years for other customers, one of whom had been instrumental in us securing the contract with Les Machines. Anyway, I thought, a couple of days away from all the paperwork would probably do me good. I made a note for Theresa to send a thank you letter and a bottle of quality brandy to the contracts manager who'd had recommended us to Les Machines.

On Tuesday, I received a call from my solicitor confirming he'd received the transfer of monies from the sale of my apartment and had released the keys to the new owners. I made a bank transfer for the remaining amount required to complete the deposit for Birchwood House Farm. The email forwarded by Gainsborough & Partners detailed the amount required plus their charges, including a list of disbursements which seemed endless. This however, was not the time for nitpicking. With something like this, I always kept the bigger picture at the forefront of my mind. It was, for me anyway, the only way. Do all the calculations, then if you're confident, set your plans in motion and like hell, just go for it.

Chapter 11

I spent Tuesday evening with Carol at her house. Being homeless, she said it was the least she could do. Her sense of humour, as always, was on form.

It was the following morning as I walked back into the bedroom after taking my usual shower, I remembered I had no clean clothes, nothing decent to wear. Everything: shirts, jeans, underwear (clean or otherwise) – I'd chucked them all into the large wash basket at the flat and told Barry to put it with all the other gear on the truck. Oh well, I thought, it'll be another quick visit to Marks & Spencer before starting the day. However, I was wrong. Carol had collected all my clothes, which she'd washed, ironed and hung in the wardrobe.

"Carol, I'd just thought what the hell I was going to wear today. Thanks! My shirts have never looked so good."

"I knew you wouldn't think about anything as unimportant as clothes. Good job I'm around don't you think? Oh and by the way, this fell out from one of your jacket pockets."

It was the copy of the letter, or more precisely, the note I'd intended to bury in the local park somewhere. I'd almost forgotten all about the incident in Paris and my meeting with Catherine at the Emperor's Palace the other evening.

"What is it, Michael, some secret code?"

That was canny, I thought. I was tempted to explain everything but decided against it, for the moment anyway.

"Just something I found in the papers I brought back with me from Paris. I'd obviously picked it up by mistake somewhere when I was over there."

"Do you want to keep it?"

"I think I'd better, for the time being anyway. It might be important to someone, you never know."

"Well, today you become the proud owner of Birchwood House Farm, and tomorrow is your birthday, so what have you got planned in the way of celebrations?"

I hadn't planned anything. With the events in Paris, the new contract with Les Machines, moving house and the offices, I guess there just hadn't been room in my head to think about anything else.

"I have to be honest. I haven't planned anything Carol. Next week though we'll all go for a meal somewhere: you, Theresa, Bernard and all the drivers. We'll go one night next week. What do you think?"

"I think that's a brilliant idea but Theresa and I have already thought of that and it's all been planned for this evening: eight o'clock at the Rajnagar restaurant. You can wear the new suit I've bought you as one of your birthday presents."

Sliding back one of the doors of the wardrobe, she revealed a dark blue, very smart looking two-piece suit.

"It's a day early, Michael, but what the hell, happy birthday."

I'd got clean clothes this morning, and a brand new suit ready for this evening. There was more than one reason I loved this girl.

I arrived at the office at just turned 8am. The new girls were there, busy helping pack away all the files, papers and various stationery items. Theresa had arranged for one of them to man the telephones, taking all the messages and confirming with everyone who'd forgotten the recent letter we'd sent advertising our relocation to

Birchwood House Farm on the 28th May. It seemed like organised chaos but at least it was organised. Theresa was proving, as always, a good choice of business partner.

I picked up the cup of coffee handed to me by Louise, the second of our new additions, and took this out to the rear car park, together with my mobile and cigarettes. I sat there in the warm sunshine, which was continuing to disprove everyone's theory that we were in for another wet and useless summer.

I lit a cigarette just as my mobile rang. It was Bill Carter, my accountant.

"Michael I don't know what you've done to deserve this and to be honest I don't understand it at all, but I've just received a letter from our friends at the Revenue confirming they've posted you a cheque for £26,358 as a refund of your last half year's tax payment."

"Is that normal? I don't think I've ever had any refund before. Certainly not one anywhere near that amount. You know we're moving offices today. Have they confirmed where they've sent the cheque?"

"They're sending it to your offices at Birmingham – posted yesterday, according to the letter."

"Thanks for letting me know. Our post should have arrived by now. I'll go and see if it's there, and thanks for the news. The cash will certainly be needed."

"Okay, Michael, but take a tip from me and put half of it to one side. Should they discover they've made a mistake, and to be honest, I cannot for the life of me see where on earth they've got their calculations from, they can demand a refund, so be careful."

"I will. Thanks, Bill."

Bloody hell, I thought. All clean shirts this morning, a new suit and now a cheque from none other than her Majesty for £26,000 or so, and it's not even my birthday until tomorrow.

I quickly extinguished my cigarette and went back into the

office to go through the post which had just arrived. There it was: the unmistakable tan-coloured envelope usually so dreaded by us all. But not this time, I hoped. I opened the envelope and there it was: a cheque made in the sum of £26,358. I could use this for the plans I'd got for converting one of the barns into two one-bedroom cottages. According to our local estate agents, I would be able to rent them out for around £550 to £650 per month. I'd had three quotes for the conversion, the best being one for just under £30,000, to include all materials and labour. The barn, a two-storey outbuilding, was structurally sound. The work required to turn this into two cottages, I'd envisaged, consisted mainly of dry lining the walls, updating the drainage, fitting two bathrooms and two kitchens, decorating, and supplying some basic furnishings and white goods for the kitchens. With doing some of the work myself it was possible I could get it all completed for around £25,000.

As all these plans were running through my mind I received another call on my mobile, this time from my solicitor. Having received all the monies from Barclays Bank, completion on the purchase of Birchwood House Farm had now taken place. I could collect the keys from their offices whenever I was ready.

I went out to the garages at the rear of the depot and told Jim, Ray and Barry they could start delivering all my gear to Birchwood House, and to collect the keys from my solicitors on their way over there.

"Then you'll need to get back here and start loading everything from the office."

It was exciting, and with the unexpected windfall this morning I was on a high, keen to get everything up and running. The refund this morning, I thought, dispels any doubts I may have had about the status of Catherine McKenzie. I remembered she'd asked me when my birthday was. Had this been her way of confirming her association with MI6? At the moment I just couldn't think of another explanation.

I wanted to check a couple of things on my computer before I switched off, ready for loading into the vans. I went back into the office, sat down at my desk and clicked into the main menu. There were a couple of messages in my Hotmail account. I clicked into the inbox. The first message was some spam mail which I immediately deleted. The second was from Catherine McKenzie and had the subject heading: Happy Birthday. I clicked in.

CatherineMcKenzie@Codemail.com has sent you a secure email. To read it please visit the following web page.

A web link was listed. I clicked and was immediately transferred to a website for an email encryption service.

Your message has been protected. You must answer the following question to retrieve this. You are limited to three incorrect answers.

Question: Who had some very unusual clothes made for them?

I looked again at the question. I typed in The Emperor. *The Emperor's New Clothes*, the book by Hans Christian Andersen, and the name of the restaurant Catherine used as our meeting place last week. The message appeared.

Happy Birthday for tomorrow, Michael. Hope you find the present from HM useful.
*   I need to see you though. VERY IMPORTANT. Still better we're not seen together. Please meet my partner George at the electrical department in John Lewis, Touchwood.*
10.15am Friday 30th May.
Regards,
Catherine

Now my feelings of elation and excitement were mixed with intrigue – what did Catherine want? I was too busy now to give the message much thought. I'd find out on Friday.

The big move that afternoon went surprisingly well. We'd managed to transport most of the furniture and office equipment safely to Birchwood House Farm. Two of the four telephone lines were up and running and the office was slowly beginning to take shape. The bulk of the operation was completed by 9pm. We decided it was too late to keep to our evening celebration meal at the Rajnagar so I telephoned the restaurant, made my apologies and promised we'd make another booking soon. I then ordered the biggest takeaway ever.

There were nine of us in all: Theresa and her husband Bernard; the two new additions to our office staff, Louise and Melissa; the drivers of the day, Jim, Ray and Barry; and Carol and me. I doubted Birchwood House Farm had experienced such a rude awakening in all of its 150 or so years' existence. We enjoyed the well-earned takeaway and a dozen bottles of red wine. I couldn't help thinking that when the office is up and running with all the extra business from Les Machines, I just might move my personal accommodation over to one of the cottages I'd planned. I'd need some peace and quiet now and again surely.

Suddenly, everyone started singing Happy Birthday. Carol walked into the lounge we'd all taken over for our celebrations carrying a cake she'd bought for me. It had just turned midnight and I realised I had just reached the grand old age of 37. Everyone had drunk far too much to risk driving back home, so without exception, everyone stayed and continued to drink, joke and eventually fall asleep. The following morning I woke and out of habit began to look for the clock, always on the right-hand side of the bed, on the cabinet next to the lamp. What was the time? I couldn't be late at the office – too much to do. Then I realised I was already at the office, Birchwood House Farm. I lifted myself up and realised I was on the very edge of the mattress and about to fall. I pulled myself back wondering how I'd made it to the bedroom. For the life of me I couldn't remember. My mind was a blank after Carol had presented me with the birthday cake, complete with thirty-seven lit candles. I could recall absolutely nothing. The last time this happened was after celebrating Bill the accountant's stag night. I woke the following morning with little or no memory of the final few hours of the previous night.

Carol walked into the bedroom.

"Come on, Michael, clean clothes over there on the chair, toiletries and towels in the bathroom and breakfast will be ready in ten minutes."

Not completely sure I wanted anything to eat, and amazed at how Carol had not only survived last night but recovered so quickly to organise everything, including me, I staggered out of bed.

"What time is it?"

"Just turned 7am and you're the first to rouse yourself this morning. Soon as you've finished getting yourself sorted out I'll go and wake the others."

I staggered to the bathroom, showered, shaved, then returned to the bedroom and dressed. How I survived pre-Carol, I had no idea. Breakfast was cereal and coffee. I had not yet organised a cooker for the kitchen, but I doubt I could have tackled anything else. Certainly anything remotely suggesting eggs and bacon would not have been attempted.

Over the next hour everyone had risen and, among a chorus of moans and groans and several promises of, never to again, muffled only by the fizz of Alka Selza's our new office was up and running. Birchwood House Farm had been reborn.

Chapter 12

The first day at Birchwood House Farm went quite well. With Theresa's planning and the much needed extra help from our new recruits the new office was beginning to take shape. The new assistant mechanic had started with us and with his help, Gordon was beginning to sort out the barn which we'd allocated for the servicing of our trucks. The day seemed to fly past and it was only later that I began to feel the effects of our celebrations the night before. An early night seemed to put things right for me. After a very light breakfast and dressed in the new suit Carol had bought me, I made my way to town and the meeting requested by Catherine. After parking my car in the multi-storey car park, I made my way to the John Lewis store at the front of the town's recently constructed shopping centre.

I needed a microwave, it was only 10.15am so I decided to look through the different models on offer. After all, the electrical department was where I'd rather conveniently been asked to meet George, Catherine's partner. After spending a few minutes glancing at the appliances on offer (and being somewhat confused by all the technical explanations and different options available, explained to me in detail by the very pleasant assistant standing at my side), I decided to leave this particular task to Theresa or Carol. I was happy to admit I was out of my depth on this one.

I wandered around the department wondering what sort of guy Catherine's partner would be. When you meet someone it sometimes comes as a surprise when you're introduced to their choice of partner. The surprise this time was a little more than usual. I worked hard not to show this as the tall and very attractive lady came over to me and introduced herself.

"Michael, isn't it?" She held out her hand. "My name is Georgina. Catherine asked me to meet you here. There's a restaurant on the first floor – how about we get ourselves a coffee and find somewhere I can explain a few things."

I didn't feel awkward at all, just keen to show absolutely no suggestion of surprise, but also conscious of not overdoing things.

We ascended the escalator to the second floor. I got two coffees and walked over to the table Georgina had chosen near the balcony overlooking the main shopping centre.

"Do you and Catherine live locally?" I asked, trying to break the ice.

"Worcester, Michael."

Anxious to get things underway I came straight to the point.

"Tell me, what is it Catherine wants from me?"

"Firstly, Michael, I'm sure Catherine has explained to you the need to be cautious. We have to be absolutely sure you're not being followed. Catherine is at a hotel, just at the end of the high street. The only way we can make sure you're not followed is for me to follow you. Do you have your mobile?"

"Yes."

I took the phone from my pocket.

"Let me have it. It's just possible it's tagged. I need to hang onto this until after your meeting. You take this one."

Georgina handed me a replacement mobile.

"Do you work with Catherine? Are you employed by our security services as well?"

"No, I help Catherine with her journalism occasionally, but

don't get involved with her work very much at all. I'm just giving her a helping hand at the moment, like you."

I somehow wished my involvement here was as simple as that, but I had the feeling the situation was about to get more complicated than simply lending a helping hand.

"Catherine is at the George Hotel at the end of the high street. I need you to walk out of here, turn left, then out of the shopping centre at the top of the high street. Cross over to Poplar Road, through the arcade to Mell Square. Then back here, through the shopping centre again and out at the exit by The Manor House. Walk over to the other side of the high street and carry on to the main entrance of the George Hotel. Walk through the main reception area, turn through the first door on the left and there is a sign pointing to rooms 100–186. Walk down the corridor and up the stairs at the end of the corridor facing you. Go up to the first floor, turn left and room 162 is the third on your left. That's where Catherine will be. Now if I see you're being followed at any time I will call you. Don't answer the phone. It'll be the only call you'll receive. Simply turn back, go to your car and leave. I'll make sure your phone is returned within a couple of hours."

I looked at Georgina.

"Okay, I'm on my way."

"After the meeting with Catherine come back here and we'll swap phones again."

Picking up the mobile Georgina had just handed me, I got up from the table, took the escalator to the ground floor and walked out of the department store into the main shopping centre. I turned left, walked over to the high street, into Poplar Road and through the arcade to Mell Square. Continuing with Georgina's instructions, I walked back to the high street, through the shopping centre again and out at the exit next to The Manor House. I turned right and walked towards my destination, the George Hotel. As I approached the entrance to the hotel I heard the jingle sound of a mobile. I stopped and was about to turn back when I realised this had come from a mobile belonging to a woman walking a couple of yards behind me. I carried on, went through the main entrance of the hotel, walked down to the reception area and through the door marked 'Rooms 100–186', up the stairs at the end of the corridor, and left to room 162. I knocked on the door, which was opened by Catherine McKenzie.

"Thank you for coming, Michael."

I glanced around the room. There was a lady's coat and large blue headscarf draped over the chair at the side of the bed and unless I was mistaken, a pair of enormous sunglasses. On the dressing table was a laptop, opened but not switched on, two mobile phones, a pack of twenty Silk Cut King Size cigarettes and a lighter.

"Did the letter you asked me to post arrive, Catherine?"

"It did but unfortunately someone got to the photographs before us. All we have is a dead body, but no negatives or papers."

Catherine, obviously preoccupied with her thoughts, turned to me.

"Look I know I have no right to ask you, Michael, but I need your help. Can you give me a lift to Germany in one of your trucks? I need to try to make contact with agent Snowstorm. Can you do that for me?"

"I can but tell me, why not get one of your people at MI6 to help? They're trained for this sort of thing surely, and a lot more capable of handling any possible hiccups along the way."

"Unfortunately it's not as simple as that. I'm involved with what is called a sealed operation. Only a couple of people at MI6 are aware of the operation. I can't just go back to the office and ask for assistance, so to speak. Not at the moment anyway. The operation is secret for a couple of reasons: the sensitivity of what's going on and a suspicion that someone else, possibly at MI6, is very close to uncovering the whole bloody thing. At the moment I have to work completely under my own steam and…well, you, Michael, are the only person I can think of who knows enough about what I'm involved in, and has the means of getting me to Germany under the guise of being your co-driver."

I thought for second.

"Co-driver? Have you ever driven a heavy goods vehicle?"

"No. I'll leave the driving to you. I've arranged all the necessary paperwork: HGV licence, new identity – all that will be ready tomorrow. All I need is for you to drive me there. I can't just get a flight at the moment. I'm convinced I'm being shadowed. The safest way is with a new identity and what better way than being your co-driver?"

"But if we're stopped going through customs it could create problems, Catherine. It could even jeopardise my contract with Les Machines."

"You won't be stopped, Michael. And if you are, or if anything goes wrong, I promise it won't create problems for you. I'll make sure of that. I'm working alone here but I still have access to all the usual contacts. The only difference is no one at MI6 apart from my head of department and his assistant can know anything about what I'm doing at the moment. It really is that sensitive."

I thought for a second. I had got a delivery to make next Tuesday which I'd pencilled in for myself, picking up the equipment from Liverpool and delivering to contractors just outside Hamburg. Had Catherine, with all her contacts as she described them, arranged that as well?

"I suppose you didn't have anything to do with that particular transport of equipment we have to make to Germany next Tuesday by any chance?"

"No, Michael, I didn't have a hand in that, but if you have already arranged a trip over to Germany then that would be even better. So will you help with this one? Will you give me a lift? I can't drive a heavy goods vehicle but I make great sandwiches. I smoke, like you, so no complaints from the passengers and I promise not to talk too much."

I smiled.

"I must want my bloody head looking at but okay, next Tuesday then. Where do I meet you?"

"Junction 9 off the M40, the turn off to Bicester. Pull off the motorway. I'll be in my car. George will drive it back for me."

"Next Tuesday it is then, Catherine. I'll meet you at junction 9 off the M40 at...let me see... by the time I get the equipment from the factory in Liverpool loaded up it'll be around midday, so let's say between 1.30 to 2pm."

"Now before you go, Michael, there are a couple of things I need to explain. Firstly, your mobile. It's just possible it's being tagged, so leave it at home, put it safe somewhere where nobody is going to move it. George is taking my phone with her for a couple of days' break in Spain. Anyone keeping tags on us will hopefully think you're busy at your new offices at Birchwood House and I'm taking a couple of days' break in the sun."

I somehow wished I could swap places with Georgina and take the two days' break in Spain, but I guess that option was not on offer.

"Catherine, when we get to Germany, what is your task, or shouldn't I ask?"

Catherine looked deep in thought then.

"I need to locate Snowstorm and talk to him. There's something that doesn't quite ring true about this whole business. If I'm to bring things to any sort of a successful conclusion then I need to speak to him and get to the truth over a couple of things, which at the moment, are bugging me."

After what was another mind-blowing liaison with Catherine McKenzie I walked back from the hotel and along the high street to the John Lewis department store. I took the escalator to the restaurant to collect my mobile from Georgina. As I walked towards her I had an idea.

"Georgina, do you know anything about cooking?"

"That must be one of the most romantic proposals I've had in a long time, Michael. Yes, according to Catherine my culinary skills are top-notch. She's been on at me for ages to write my own cookbook. Everybody else seems to be doing it these days. Anyway why do you ask?"

"Well, all I need, Georgina is a microwave – nothing fancy, nothing I need a degree in computer sciences to operate. Just a plain simple microwave I can use in my new kitchen capable of heating the odd Chinese or Indian meal."

Georgina laughed.

"Come on, let's see what they've got on offer here."

We walked down to the electrical department and over to the various microwave appliances on display.

"Nothing more complicated than a five-minute warm-up of a standard takeaway you say?"

"Nothing more complicated, Georgina."

"That one's a good make."

Georgina pointed to a familiar looking white box, manufactured by some company with a name I would have difficulty in pronouncing.

"Thank you! You've saved my girlfriend and business partner the task of sorting this one out for me."

I said goodbye to Georgina, went over to the assistant who had earlier tried in vain to explain the workings of the more complicated appliances on offer and confirmed my purchase of the machine Georgina had recommended.

Carrying the box under my arm and trying not to crash into too many of the shoppers walking through the arcade, I made my way to the multi-storey car park and drove back to Birchwood House. I couldn't help thinking that although Catherine and Georgina seemed two of the nicest people I'd met in a long time, I was getting myself involved in something which was unknown territory for me – not only that but bloody dangerous as well. I couldn't help wishing Catherine had kept to a simple career in journalism and not diversified her expertise to include helping our security services. But then, I thought, I'd be oblivious to everything that was going on around me. That bloody attaché case and the letter had landed me well and truly in the middle of something I was struggling to get my head around.

Chapter 13

I jet-washed the truck I was going to use on Tuesday for, among other things, delivery of the underpinning equipment ordered by Les Machines' customer in Hamburg. After the sponging down and jet-washing procedure I cleaned the inside of the cabin, the windscreen and the windows. This was something I'd insisted all the drivers would be responsible for doing. I'd made it a part of their employment contract. The cleaning area, complete with two jet systems and several drainage outlets, was situated adjacent to the barn where all the maintenance and repairs to the trucks would be carried out. Two things I'd always made sure of: first-class regular maintenance and service of all the vehicles, and a thorough cleaning of each vehicle inside and out before being used for the next delivery.

The two tanks had been filled to capacity with diesel and Gordon had made a final check of the vehicle. At just turned 8am I was on my way to the Les Machines factory in Liverpool. Their underpinning equipment was supplied in crates. The machines would then be assembled by the customer – flat-pack, so to speak. This procedure certainly suited our side of the business, making it both simple and easy for loading and unloading.

The traffic on the M6 was heavy, as usual. Always the same, I thought. I turned the radio up, took a swig from my flask and lit another cigarette, eventually arriving at the factory at just turned 11.30am. The equipment was loaded onto the truck within thirty minutes and after signing all the paperwork I was off. I hoped that this time, going south, the traffic would be lighter.

It was just turned 2pm as I approached the turn off to Bicester. I moved into the slow lane, signalled and pulled off the motorway. Parked a couple of hundred yards from the turn off was a white Lexus saloon. I pulled up in front of the vehicle and saw someone running towards my truck in the rear-view mirror. It took a few seconds for me to realise this was in fact Catherine. She pulled herself into the cabin like an experienced HGV driver. Placing two packs of Silk Cut cigarettes on the seat between a couple of large holdalls, along with a lighter, sunglasses and two flasks, she turned to me.

"Ready for the off, Michael?"

The transformation, I had to admit, was good. Sporting a pair of dark blue denim jeans, a T-shirt, a beige donkey jacket and a pair of black boots, she'd successfully transformed herself into a very convincing co-driver for MCL Carriers. Not a suggestion of make-up, and every single strand of hair had disappeared under a large red cap with a gold embossed emblem of some sort, clearly displayed at the front.

"You're obviously ready for the journey, Catherine."

"I am, and thanks again for your help."

We made Calais at just turned 6.30pm, having come through the Channel Tunnel without any of the delays I'd experienced so many times in the past. We began the journey through France towards the main route I'd be taking to Hamburg. Having made the journey dozens of times over the years I planned to stop at a guest house for the night just outside the town of Kolt before commencing the last lap of our journey. I knew the village well, and the owners of the guest house where I'd planned to stop over.

Catherine poured me a cup of coffee from one of her flasks and lit a cigarette for me.

"I wouldn't mind taking this thing through Paris. There's a few vehicles there I'd like to get my own back on, not least of all the idiot who nearly ploughed me into the pavement of Rue du Faubourg Saint-Honoré – that's if I could find the little sod."

Catherine laughed.

"I've driven through Paris myself many times, so I know what you mean. A tank or one of these things we're in right now is definitely the best mode of transport to use."

However, we bypassed Paris and were soon on the main route to Germany.

"We should make the town of Kolt by around eleven this evening, Catherine. There's a guest house I know of. I've used the place several times over the years. We can rest up there for the night. Then if we start off tomorrow at around 6am we should be in Hamburg by midday. I'll need to refuel shortly. There's a garage I normally use about another twenty minutes' drive from here."

Catherine's promise of not talking too much was right. She'd been the perfect travelling companion, I thought, as she lit another cigarette for me and poured a coffee from the flask.

"How long have you been helping MI6, or shouldn't I ask?"

"I'm not employed by MI6, but my work as a war correspondent has brought me in contact with our security services from time to time. I've helped now and again and sometimes in return for a nice tax-free bonus but that aside, I'm happy to help when I can."

"And the sunglasses?" I asked jokingly. "I take it those things aren't supplied by our security services?"

"Cheeky sod! These are my choice, and very expensive too if you don't mind."

I smiled – all women seem to have the same genetic make-up when it comes to accessories, providing they are expensive and a bit 'way out.' Those were the ones that sold.

"The code used in that letter, Catherine. What the hell did it mean?"

"Mouse was the code name of a pornographic book shop in Soho, Mickey's Images."

"So Sew O was the code for Soho. And the numbers, Catherine, were they the combination to a safe?"

"Your talents are wasted, Michael. You'd make a good James Bond."

Catherine's relaxed, friendly and down-to-earth nature made me forget at times that she was in fact working for our secret service. Not only that, but she was right in the middle of an assignment which was sensitive to say the least, as well as – I kept reminding myself – bloody dangerous.

After stopping to refuel we eventually arrived at our destination for the night: Kolt Way Guest House. I parked the truck at the rear of the property and walked through to the reception area. The owners, Mr and Mrs Phillips, told me on my last visit that they'd purchased the business ten years ago after deciding to make a life-changing decision and give up their careers as teachers at Milton Keynes Comprehensive and move to the town of Kolt – a decision they'd never regretted. Their expertise and enthusiasm had certainly created a very successful and popular business. So successful that there was just one single room available. I paid the charge and handed the keys to Catherine.

"I'm in the truck, Catherine. No problem for me, I've done it a thousand times, to be honest I can get a far better night's sleep in there than anywhere else. So you take the keys, sort yourself out and when you're ready we'll go and get something to eat."

"We can share the room if you like, Michael. No disrespect, but I think you'll have gathered by now you're not my type. And besides that, I trust you."

"And I thought you were a good judge of character, Catherine! You take the keys – I'll be fine in the truck, I've slept in that thing dozens of times. It's absolutely no problem. I'll use the shower first though, then we can go and get something to eat."

We found a small café about a quarter of a mile from the guest house. Catherine, fluent in the language of our neighbours, guided me through the menu. Thanks to her help I enjoyed an excellent meal of steak, egg and chips and not a bad few glasses of red wine – certainly a lot better than the stuff I'd blindly chosen in Paris the other week.

"When we get to Hamburg tomorrow what's the plan? Do you want me to do anything, help in any way?"

"No, just drop me off, make your delivery, then pick me up later. That reminds me, I need to update you with the phones we're using. They have a couple of extra programs which I'll explain later."

We walked back to the guest house. Catherine went to her room as I made myself comfortable in the cabin of my truck. A cigarette, and a quick listen to the radio and that was it, I was asleep.

Chapter 14

I slept well. After eight years in the haulage business I was used to the accommodation. I woke reasonably refreshed at 6.45am, poured a cup of coffee from one of Catherine's flasks – a good strong flavour even if it was cold – lit a cigarette, took a short walk from the car park and stood looking over the surrounding countryside. Not bad, but not a patch on back home, I thought. There really is no countryside in the world to compare with England. It was always the same for me when travelling abroad, whether it was business or a holiday. I couldn't wait to get back to England, even if it was raining most of the time.

We started the last lap of our journey to Hamburg at just turned 7am. The weather was good: clear, sunny, not too hot – perfect for driving. The remaining 275 miles or so to Hamburg would be a doddle. It was. We arrived just before midday.

I found a place to park just off the main road.

"Before you go let me explain the mobiles. They work just like an ordinary mobile but with a couple of added gadgets. If you need to locate my whereabouts, or vice versa, we press number one on the menu. This displays a map just like an ordinary satnav, and gives our exact locations, okay? In an emergency, press number two. This gives the same information but with the flashing red dot here at the top of the screen. That will confirm there's a problem, or danger. The main feature with these is they're ninety-nine per cent impossible to hack. If you need to speak then just use it as an ordinary mobile."

"Any idea how long you'll be or where you want me to pick you up from?"

"At the moment no. I'll use the mobile and give my location as soon as I'm ready."

"Okay, good luck! I'll see you later."

I drove off to make my delivery of the equipment for Les Machines. I put the address where I was to make the delivery into the satnav. The instructions, rather aptly I thought, were being given to me by Sean Connery. My truck had been fitted with a new satnav system a couple of days ago. I followed 007's instructions and began the last lap of my journey.

Catherine began walking down Stift Street, a typical middle-class area, and from the sound of all the children riding their bikes and playing football, she realised it must be a school holiday. Half-term probably. All the mothers would be busy attempting to get the washing, ironing, preparation of the evening meal and a thousand other tasks completed before the end of the day. Poor sods, she thought.

Continuing to walk down Stift Street, Catherine ~~was~~ *she began* planning the best way to approach Snowstorm. She was convinced this was probably going to be the last opportunity she'd get, not only to follow through her instructions from MI6 but also to try to get the answers to a couple of questions of her own. At the back of her mind she felt uneasy over a few things that just didn't seem to add up about Operation Aries.

She stopped outside number 277. This was the address where she should be able to make contact with Snowstorm. This information she'd learnt from her investigative work and as far as she knew, even MI6 were unaware of ~~this~~ *the* address. As ~~she approached~~ *approaching* the front door Catherine thought the property looked unoccupied.

She rang the bell and waited, then rang again. Still no reply. She walked round to the property next door and rang the bell. The shouting of young children from inside confirmed at least someone was at home. The door was opened by a woman with the look of a harassed middle-aged mother struggling with the day's tasks and looking forward to the end of the school holidays.

"Can I help you?"

"I have an appointment with your neighbour, next door at number 277, but there doesn't seem to be anyone at home. You don't happen to know when he'll be back do you?"

"I don't think he's coming back. He left a couple of weeks ago. I believe the property is for rent again. He said he was going abroad to start a new job."

"Did he say where?"

"No, I hardly spoke to him all the time he was living there."

"You've absolutely no idea where he's moved to? He didn't mention anything at all about where he was going?"

"No, as I've said, somewhere abroad, that's all. You could ask his girlfriend. That's if she hasn't already joined him."

Girlfriend, wondered Catherine. Could this be a lucky break?

"Do you know where I can reach her?"

"Yes, she's a teacher at one of the colleges. My daughter recognised her. She gave our neighbour's daughter some private tuition before taking some exams. Didn't even charge for her time apparently. Hold on, I've got her address somewhere."

The woman disappeared back into the house, returning two minutes later with a piece of paper.

"Here you are, this is Heidi's address."

Catherine thanked the woman for her time and walked back down Stift Street. Had Snowstorm already left the country? According to the information from her contact at MI6 he was paid the first instalment of £1 million over two weeks ago, and if he'd got wind of the negatives being stolen from Mickey's place, he just

81

might have decided to settle for that and call it a day. By a stroke of good luck, she at least had Heidi's address. Was it possible she was still living there and could it possibly be Snowstorm was hiding there as well? A lot to hope for, but only one way to find out.

After a twenty-minute taxi ride to the other side of the River Bockenheimer Anlage, Catherine asked the driver to pull up a couple of hundred yards from the address she'd been given. Walking through the main entrance Catherine *she* made her way to the third floor and over to number 37, Heidi's apartment. She rang the bell, but no reply.

Have I missed her? she *my* thought. Have they both now cleared off?

Exiting the apartment block, Catherine made her way over to a coffee house directly opposite. Getting herself a cup of coffee, she sat at one of the tables, took a small pad out of her jacket and began to write a brief note. It was risky. Would Heidi meet someone from England who was a total stranger, someone she'd never met before? And if Snowstorm was there, what would his reaction be? But this was probably as good an approach as any. Time was running out – if Snowstorm hadn't already left the country he would surely be doing so very soon. Catherine finished the note.

> *Dear Heidi,*
> *Please excuse this method of contacting you. My name is Catherine McKenzie. I need to speak to you. Can you meet me at the Alder Coffee House opposite your apartment? I am wearing jeans and a beige jacket. I shall be at the coffee house for the remainder of the afternoon.*
> *Catherine*

Returning to Heidi's apartment, Catherine posted the note through the letterbox. Returning to the coffee house, she ordered another coffee and sat down at one of the tables. Twenty minutes later a tall, fair haired woman walked into the Alder Coffee House and recognising Catherine from the description she had given in her note, came over to the table.

"My name is Heidi. To say the least, I'm intrigued by your note."

Heidi seemed to be an easy-going, very attractive twenty-something.

"Heidi. Thank you for seeing me."

"Are you connected with the college?" enquired Heidi as she sat down at the table.

"No, I'm not connected to any college. I'm from England and I'm trying to get in touch with your boyfriend Brian. Do you have any idea where I can reach him?"

"Brian's visiting his sister and brother-in-law this afternoon. We're both flying out later to our new home in Canada so this will be the last time he'll see them for a while. What's this all about anyway?"

Catherine knew enough about Snowstorm to know he had no sister living in Germany, or anywhere else for that matter. The only surviving member of his family was his mother, a rather frail seventy-six-year-old who'd recently moved into a retirement home somewhere in the Midlands. Catherine was not about to reveal this information to Heidi – if this is what she'd been told, and if Heidi believed it, then perhaps she was totally unaware of Brian's work with MI6 and therefore everything else.

Catherine continued to ad-lib her way through what she hoped would sound a plausible reason for her visit to Germany.

"Heidi I'm trying to make contact with Brian. We worked at the same organisation in London some years ago and the owner of the company, Peter Hartnel, asked me if I could make contact with Brian to see if he would be interested in taking over their operation in Ireland. Peter's planning on retiring soon and he wants to ensure he has the right people looking after the business. His own sons have been a total disappointment unfortunately. Apart from spending money and driving fast cars, they've no real interest in the business at all. I know all this is a bit of a long shot but I told Peter I'd try and make contact with Brian and at least ask him to call and talk things over.

"What work were you involved with? Has this anything to do with the job Brian's been offered in Canada?"

It seemed, thought Catherine, Heidi really did have no idea of her boyfriend's involvement with MI6. Either that or she was continuing to put on a good act.

"The company makes parts for computers. A couple of years ago they developed a system, which I wont bore you with the details of, but a system which has the potential of completely revolutionising the computer industry.

The organisation we worked for have come up with an offer I'm sure Brian would be interested in. Peter wants to offer Brian a position within the organisation I am sure he'll wish to grab with both hands. He'll know all about what I'm referring to, I just need the opportunity to speak with him, that's all."

"At the moment Brian is visiting his sister at Eurotheum apartments, number 47."

Catherine believed Heidi was telling what she thought to be the truth.

"Maybe I'll be able to catch up with him before you both leave. You're flying out this evening you say?"

"Yes, 10.15 tonight, from Frankfurt airport."

"Do you have any idea when Brian will be back from visiting his sister?"

"It'll be later this evening. He'll probably want to drop in at the Destino club and say goodbye to some of his friends first, and probably have a few drinks with them as well."

Catherine thanked Heidi for her help and left the Alder Coffee House. Things were not as they seemed. She felt more and more uneasy about Operation Aries. The address Heidi had given her at number 47 Eurotheum apartments was in fact a so-called safe house, used by MI6. She took out her mobile – she needed to contact Michael. She hoped her suspicions were wrong, but if she was correct the situation would completely change everything. She didn't yet know the best way to handle things from here, apart from continuing to try to make contact with Brian. Catherine's instinct told her she was being used, but why? And more importantly, by whom?

Chapter 15

I'd completed the delivery of Les Machines' underpinning equipment to their customer and was halfway through a coffee and cigarette when the mobile Catherine had given me rang. I looked at the screen. It gave Catherine's location: Alder Coffee House, Medekstrasse. The green light at the top of the screen was flashing.

I went back to the truck and put the information into the satnav which confirmed this was the other side of the river from where I'd left Catherine. It took just twenty minutes to reach Medekstrasse, but another half an hour to park. Finding a convenient spot to park a 7.5 ton truck was rather more difficult than the normal mode of transport. I walked over to the main high street and spotted Catherine looking in the window of one of the shops.

"How did your meeting go with Snowstorm? Everything sorted out?"

"Unfortunately not. I spoke to his girlfriend who's given me a couple of addresses where I might find him so I need to check those out. We need to move quite fast as well. Snowstorm will immediately see through the excuse I gave his girlfriend for my wanting to meet up with him. By the way, where did you park, Michael?"

"Found a place at the rear of the Reme Supermarket, just around the corner from here."

"Will your truck be okay there for a while?"

"I think so, but it might be an idea to check it out if we're going to be tied up for a while. These mobiles are very good by the way. Saves having to stop and talk if you're driving and the pictures are excellent."

"Yes, there are a couple of other gadgets which I'll explain to you in a minute."

Catherine wanted the other rucksack she'd left under the front seat of the truck so we walked round to the back of the Reme Supermarket where I'd parked.

"Ask the guy over there, Catherine, if it's okay for us to leave it here for a while. I don't speak the language, as you know."

Catherine walked over to one of the guys I'd pointed to. He looked like one of the security people working at the supermarket. Catherine returned confirming it was okay to leave the truck where I'd parked it but we'd need to move it before 9pm when the supermarket closed.

"I need my other rucksack, Michael. I left it under the front seat."

"Okay, I'll get it for you."

I walked towards the truck and pressed the auto lock release. The explosion that followed was deafening – the force from the blast swept both of us several yards across the pavement. Debris was in the air – bits of metal and every other type of material that had once been part of my truck would soon be crashing down on us, like missiles in a war zone.

I got up and instinctively grabbed Catherine by her arm and threw her to the side of one of the two enormous garbage skips being used by the store. Pushing Catherine into the side of the container, I grabbed a sheet of plywood which had been left propped at the side of one of the containers. I held this over us as the shower of debris rained down, hitting the shield like a hailstorm.

The twisted metal that had once been my transport was

engulfed in flames and belching black smoke. I looked round to see if anyone had been caught in the hailstorm of metal fragments from the explosion so obviously intended for us. I could see no one. The security guard Catherine had been speaking to a few moments before was running from the rear doors of the delivery area of the supermarket, as were several other people.

It was time go.

"Catherine, let's get the hell out of here."

We ran back down one of the side streets leading to the main high street. The explosion would have been heard for several miles around. People were running towards the scene, others were just standing, and some with more sense were running in the opposite direction. Not wishing to look conspicuous we stopped running and just carried on walking. I heard the sound of sirens: police, ambulance and fire engines. We needed to get as far away from the area as possible, then we could decide what the hell to do next. After about thirty minutes we found ourselves walking down a path off the main high street which led to a park area. There was a lake and some benches and as far as I could see, just one elderly couple walking their dog along the surrounding footpath.

We sat on one of the benches. For the first time since the explosion Catherine spoke – her hands shaking, she wiped the dust off her face and eyelashes.

"Michael thanks for that back there, you probably saved my life. It's not fair to get you involved any deeper in all this. We have contacts over here. I can ring for help now. Our contacts will arrange to get you to a safe house and London will organise a return flight for you."

"And what will you do?"

"Whatever I decide to do, I know I've very little time left if I've any chance of making contact with Snowstorm. According to his girlfriend they're due to fly out at 10.15pm tonight to start their journey to Canada. That gives me just a few hours to make one last attempt at finding him, and to be honest I'm not at all hopeful. Snowstorm's girlfriend, probably without knowing it, has set me up. She'd obviously been told to give me the address of where I would find her boyfriend. What she wasn't aware of was my connection with MI6. The address she gave me is one of our safe houses – one I actually used myself a couple of years ago. But Snowstorm just might be there and I need to find out. Then there is the possibility of two other places: the Destino club, and finally, Frankfurt airport."

"Catherine, if the address Heidi has given you belongs to your organisation then I don't understand. I thought you said Snowstorm was a rogue agent, blackmailing your organisation for £2 million for the location of those negatives and papers he found in Iraq."

"You're right, and that's what I'm trying to make sense of. I've had my doubts about this operation from day one. The more I'm stumbling across, the more I'm convinced it's not as it seems. I want a bit more time before making any decision on this."

"Do you have any photographs of this Snowstorm character?"

Before asking the question I had decided I was not leaving Catherine to work through all this on her own.

"What for?"

"Well, you go and check the address Heidi gave you and I'll check out the Destino club. If there's still no luck we'll meet up at Frankfurt airport for one last go."

"Are you sure about this?"

"You may think this strange but some cheeky bastard has just blown up one of my trucks – before, I may add, I'd even had time to arrange for the new logo to be painted on it. Last week some joyrider nearly ploughed me into the pavement stones of Rue du Faubourg and the poor sod who took over my room at the Hotel Campanile has been murdered. If nothing else, I think I deserve the chance to at least see one of these insane individuals put away. Don't you think?"

"I think you're totally mad, Michael. But I'm very grateful for the offer of help."

Catherine took a photograph from her jacket pocket and handed it to me.

"This is Snowstorm, real name Brian Ford. 5'7" tall, slim build, very dark brown, almost black hair, green eyes and walks with a limp – only slightly, but it is noticeable. And this, Michael, is a 13mm Gyrojet handgun complete with silencer – and before you say anything, don't. It's just a safeguard. The safety catch is here. Just press this down to release the mechanism. It's fully loaded, and you have twelve rounds. Don't try to remove the silencer. Without that you'll probably do more harm to your eardrums than whoever you're aiming at. This is the address where I'm off to. Give it one hour, Michael. If you have no luck, press green on the mobile. I'll do the same and we'll meet up at the airport, no later than 9pm. The Destino club is about four miles from here. Take a taxi. My location is about six miles in the opposite direction. Should either of us hit lucky, we press the red button, okay?

One last thing, Michael, if you do happen to see Brian, don't let him out of your sight. I know that's a rather obvious request but just press red and whatever it takes, keep him with you."

Chapter 16

I took a taxi to the Destino club, which from first impressions, looked an inviting sort of place – as it happened, one of the best hostelries I'd visited for a long time. The bar area wasn't busy. Looking at my watch I suspected it would be packed in another couple of hours if the places back home were anything to go by. I was aware though that I had just under an hour to look for this character, Snowstorm. Then it would be Frankfurt airport.

I ordered myself a pint of lager by pointing to the pump and making it clear I did not speak German. "No spreche der Deutsch," followed by an impression of downing a pint of their advertised brew seemed to do the trick. I looked around the bar area but there was no sign of Brian. Carrying my pint I walked out of the bar through the patio doors to the gardens at the rear of the premises. I sat at one of the benches at the far end where I would be able to see everyone going in and coming out. It was a warm evening and although the sun was now lower in the sky, it was still illuminating this area of our planet, for a while longer, I thought.

Catherine arrived by taxi at the Eurotheum apartments. Aware the events so far today were beginning to show quite a different aspect to Operation Aries, her uneasiness about the situation brought to the fore the survival instincts and training techniques taught to her by the SAS. Pushing down the safety catch of the pistol she was carrying, she put this into her jacket pocket and ascended the steps of the apartment block before walking over to number 47. She rang the bell and waited. After a couple of minutes and two more attempts at the bell Catherine pushed on the door, which opened.

Entering the hallway, she pulled the pistol from her jacket pocket and held it at her side. The door at the far end of the hallway opened. The silhouette of a large stocky guy appeared, somehow looking even more menacing by the dim light of the street lamps behind him coming through from the lounge windows. Using all the techniques she'd been trained for, Catherine dropped to the floor, managing to miss the two shots fired at her. At the same time, the one shot she fired went cleanly through the forehead of her would-be assailant, killing him instantly.

Getting up, Catherine walked towards the crumpled heap which lay before her. She was aware there was little need to check for life. She knew the bullet she'd fired would have done the job but Catherine bent down and felt for a pulse, which confirmed the obvious. She continued to look around the apartment, checking each room and looking through the cupboards in the kitchen and drawers of the cabinet in the lounge. Everything was clean, absolutely clean. There was nothing here – aside from confirmation that Operation Aries was not as she'd been briefed.

Taking the mobile out of her pocket, Catherine pressed the red button. A sharp pain at the back of her head was followed by blue and silver flashing lights. Catherine slumped to the floor.

The signal on my mobile told me Catherine was either in trouble or had got our man. I walked out of the Destino club and hailed a taxi to take me to Eurotheum apartments. We pulled up outside the apartment block, a typically panel-built high rise block constructed from the most unimaginative blue and beige coloured panels which somehow looked even more depressing by the onset of dusk.

I paid the fare and walked over to the main entrance. I had no need to use the buzzer, a young couple just leaving the building held the door for me. I slipped through to the main hall and took the stairs to number 47.

I rang the bell and waited. There was no reply. I rang again, wondering if I'd got the wrong apartment. Was it 37? Or 47?

Struggling to get into my inside jacket pocket, I pulled out the paper Catherine had given me. It was number 47. Had Catherine left already?

Remembering the earlier attempt to blast us off the face of the earth and the fate of the guest who'd taken over my room at the Hotel Campanile, I was becoming more aware of the very real danger which surrounded us. I had no hesitation in attempting to force the door – an exercise I quickly discovered was not needed.

The door opened without effort. I entered the apartment holding the pistol Catherine had supplied me with. At the end of the hallway I saw the body of a man slumped in the doorway to what I assumed was the lounge. I walked slowly over to the crumpled heap to check him out. He was definitely a goner, which didn't surprise me, seeing the bullet hole in the centre of his forehead. The apartment seemed empty and I wondered if I was too late. Had Catherine bought it as well?

The whole series of events over the past couple of weeks was running through my mind. My near-death experience in Paris. The assassination of the guest who'd taken over my room at the Hotel Campanile. The attempt to blow both Catherine and myself off the face of the earth only a couple of hours previously. It was obvious we were entangled in something which was becoming increasingly dark and sinister. Now the reality of all that was staring me in the face. I couldn't help wondering if I would see Carol again. Would Catherine and I get out of all this alive?

All these thoughts were running through my mind as I checked out the bedrooms, the kitchen and the bathroom, then stepping over the crumpled heap in the doorway, I walked through into the lounge. I saw Catherine lying face down on the floor. I went over to her. Kneeling beside her, I checked her pulse. She was alive – a small amount of blood at the back of her head made it obvious she'd been knocked unconscious from behind. I went to the bathroom, grabbed a couple of towels and held them under the tap. As I returned Catherine was beginning to pick herself up.

"What the hell happened? Are you alright? Here, take this towel, sit down for a minute."

"No time, we need to get out of here, Michael."

Grabbing her mobile and holding onto me, Catherine unsteadily got to her feet. We walked out of the apartment and as we crossed the landing, I noticed two cameras overlooking the area. Then, as we descended to the main hall, I noticed another one positioned over the main door.

We walked out of the apartment building down the stone steps to the pavement. I wondered how the hell we'd ever get back to England. My truck had been blown to a thousand pieces and both of us had now been recorded on cameras exiting apartment 47, where the body of some guy lay with a bullet hole through his forehead. Surely it was just a matter of time before we'd be arrested? The only plus, I thought to myself, was that we were both still alive...for the moment.

"What's the next move, Catherine? The airport?"

"No need. I checked earlier – there's no flight to Canada tonight, or any other destination on route. We're being led in the wrong direction and it would appear, by more than one person."

We walked across the road and into a passageway leading down to the rear of a restaurant. Catherine sat on one of the bins, holding the back of her head, trying to ease the pain from the blow she'd received.

"I need to check out Heidi's apartment at Medekstrasse and see if there is any sign of Brian or Heidi. I very much doubt there will be, but it's the only chance we have left – at least for tonight. Then I'll make a call and get us some help to get back to England."

"Help from your contacts over here?"

"Yes, Michael. Don't worry, our security services have a pretty good network of operatives in Germany. But first let's make a visit to Heidi's apartment."

A ten-minute taxi ride later, we arrived at Elbo Street. Our taxi pulled up outside the apartment block. We ascended the stone stairway to the third floor and walked over to Heidi's apartment. Stuck to the door, just over the letterbox, was a scribbled note which appeared to have been written on a piece of torn envelope.

Keys to the apartment at the Alder Coffee House.
Regards,
Heidi

My lock-breaking technique was required this time. After three attempts the door opened. The apartment was empty. Looking around the place it became obvious Brian and Heidi had been successful in laying a false trail for us, enabling them to make their disappearing act. We both searched through the apartment but nothing had been left. All the cupboards, drawers and cabinets had been completely cleared. We descended the stairway as Catherine made her call for assistance to get us out of Germany and back to England.

"What size jacket are you? We'll both need a change of clothes and a place to hide away for a while."

"I take a forty-two long."

Catherine was busy relaying this information, which I couldn't help feeling was totally insignificant, considering everything going on around us.

"Right, Michael. We have a place for tonight. And tomorrow, with a bit of luck, things should be in place, ready for our journey back home. We'll need another taxi. The place we'll be staying at tonight is just outside Hamburg, about a forty-minute drive from here."

A good thirty minutes or so into our journey I was becoming more concerned by the headlights from a car behind us, which unless I was very much mistaken, had been following us since driving away from Eurotheum apartments. I reckoned it could be the guy who'd knocked Catherine unconscious. After realising she'd managed to send a message on her mobile seconds before, he'd more than likely decided to hide, either somewhere in the apartment or close by, and then follow us. All these thoughts were running through my mind. I turned to Catherine, who was still massaging the back of her neck.

In a low voice, I conveyed my plan of action.

"We can't be more than a few minutes away from this safe house of yours. I'm going to ask the driver to pull over. I want to check out the car behind us. You carry on, let me know when you're there."

Catherine was about to say something but I interrupted. I'd made up my mind. It was time for me to take control. Things were beginning to bug me to say the least. However big or sensitive this operation was, it was time to fight back. Sod everything else. It was, as I saw things, the only chance either of us would have to get back to England. And get back I was determined to do.

"Just do as you're told. Let me know when you're there, press the green button on this contraption and I'll meet up with you."

I asked the driver to pull over. I got out of the cab and began walking back down the lane as he drove off. The car following us began to slow down, then stopped. I was right – he had been following us.

I found myself standing on a deserted country lane with no street lamps. I hoped this was not going to turn out to be my final resting place. There was a full moon, which I thought may or may not be very helpful. The silver-blue illumination made an eerie outline of the tree-lined area. It was *I thought* a somewhat ~~theatrical scene~~, reminiscent of a murder mystery movie. However, I was determined I was not about to play the part of the victim. Walking slowly towards the glaring headlights, I could hear the engine still ticking over like an angry predator preparing to pounce.

Then I saw the driver's window silently lowering, and in the shadows I caught a glimpse of a pistol pointing towards me. I made a dive to the ground. As I landed two bullets hit the pavement next to me, showering splinters of stone over my head. Holding my pistol in both hands I fired six shots in succession, and waited. I heard the sound of the pistol that had been aimed at me a few seconds earlier fall to the ground.

This was the first time I had used any firearm. If I'd been successful, there just had to have been help from somewhere. My faith in the existence of a creator seemed to return. I picked myself up and walked slowly towards the car. The headlights were still glaring, the engine still ticking over. The driver, however, had just made his last journey. There were two bullet holes in the driver's door. I reckoned the other four at least had made the target, which had removed the best part of my adversary's head to the back seat. This, and more blood than I would ever wish to see again, made a sickening picture I'd not forget in a hurry.

I leaned into the car, switched off the engine and the lights, and began to walk back in the direction of our taxi. After a couple of minutes the mobile rang, displaying the location of the safe house where Catherine and I would be hiding away for a while. Fifteen minutes later I reached our destination. It was a peaceful looking tree-lined country lane with an assortment of differently styled cottages and bungalows. Catherine was waiting for me. We both walked down the lane to a small cottage. I assumed this was where we would be staying until all the arrangements had been made to get us back home.

"Was the car following us?"

"Yes, but it was his last journey."

"When we get back to England we'll need to make a full report. I'll make sure everything's okay for you. Come on, I think we both deserve a break. We have a change of clothes in here and I can run a bath. We'll be contacted as soon as our papers are ready – new identities, passports and tickets for our flight. It'll probably take a day to get all that together so my guess is we'll be on our way back to England sometime Friday."

After Catherine, I had a soak in the bath. It felt good. I got out and put on one of the towelling dressing gowns, apparently left for us, laying down on the bed I assumed was for me. Catherine came into the bedroom with two cups of coffee.

"I've searched everywhere but couldn't find anything stronger I'm afraid."

"I'm sorry. I didn't realise this was your bedroom. I'll drink this and get out of your way."

Catherine sat on the side of the bed. I could see blood on the collar of her dressing gown.

"Is that still causing you problems?"

"A bit sore but I've had worse."

I went to the bathroom, picked up a tube of antiseptic cream I'd noticed earlier and returned to the bedroom. Squeezing some of the cream from the tube onto my fingers, I began to massage this into the cuts and bruises on Catherine's neck and shoulders.

"That should help. Now I'll get out of your way and let you get some sleep."

"You don't have to go. In fact I'd really rather you stayed with me tonight."

I noticed how shaken Catherine looked.

"I'll sleep on the floor over here then. Chuck us a pillow over and one of those blankets."

"Michael, just get into bed. As you're already aware, you're not my type. Get into bed. I just need someone to be with me."

"Alright, Catherine. We keep our hands to ourselves is what you're trying to say. Correct?"

Catherine smiled. I don't know where my sudden burst of comedy originated from – probably a reaction in an attempt to dispel the after-effects of the day's almost fatal events. Whatever, it did the trick. Catherine seemed to relax, and a hint of a smile remained. I got into bed and put my arm around this very beautiful, elegant and capable woman, who I knew just needed a few moments of reassurance. We laid there, in perfect silence. I guessed Catherine, who was staring at the ceiling, wanted to talk.

"Go on, Catherine, tell me your thoughts."

"I'm thinking my work as a war correspondent has taken me to Chechnya, Bosnia, Afghanistan and Iraq, among other places. I've witnessed first-hand, some of the most awful and unbelievable demonstrations of man's inhumanity to man. But this evening, back there at Eurotheum apartments, I wondered what the hell it was all about. I began to question what I was doing. I always had at the back of my mind the thought that one day I could quite easily end up in some out of the way place with a bullet through my head and a shallow grave for my final resting place. This operation though, Operation Aries – there's something more behind it. I know that, and I don't like the feel of it at all. When you see all the devastation caused by war, you question everything, even your own existence. But do you know what the most sickening part about all that is, Michael? It's seeing the vultures flying over the remnants of all that remains, looking for their opportunities. I have a horrible feeling that's just what's happening now. Operation Aries. It's not what I thought."

Not knowing quite how, or perhaps not wanting to delve further into Catherine's thoughts about Operation Aries, I chose what I thought would be a slightly speedier but nevertheless acceptable way to continue our discussion.

"I've never served in the forces, Catherine but I had an uncle who did. He was in the Falklands and Northern Ireland for a while but he never talked about it, never said a word."

"That's one of the trademarks, Michael. When you've seen the inhumanity of war, you question everything, it's as if....as if the answers you know deep down to be true are just too difficult to accept. You end up locking them away somewhere, behind shadows of your own creation."

I leaned over and gave Catherine a kiss.

"We've got a busy day tomorrow, and remember we're all part of the same journey. I certainly can't explain it. But with all your expertise you should avoid all this secret service work and concentrate on your work as a journalist and presenter. Make your thoughts known. You have all the talent in the world to do that."

"I will one day, one day quite soon. Georgina needs an operation and the best chance of success is for her to have the treatment she needs in America. We're not exactly destitute but the cost of the operation and all the subsequent treatment will come to well over £200,000. The plan is to sell the house and downsize to a place in St Ives, Cornwall. That's the plan anyway. So maybe next year I'll arrange my life differently."

I felt Catherine pull me closer. It felt good, but...

"Now before I'm tempted to make a complete bloody fool of myself, Catherine, we go to sleep, right?"

"Right, Michael, we go to sleep."

Chapter 17

"Your drink, Sir David."

"Thank you. Have you seen Peter this evening?"

"I understand he's in the restaurant, sir. Shall I ask him to come through when he's finished?"

"Please, if you would, Andrew."

St Michael's in Bridge Street, Westminster, was without question one of the most exclusive clubs in the capital. It had been the retreat for members of royalty, both here and around the world. Prime ministers, cabinet ministers, members of parliament, heads of banks and chiefs of industry from every corner of the globe had sought sanctuary within its walls for over 150 years. Membership of St Michael's, outside the aforementioned categories, would be virtually impossible. During its illustrious history, the most famous and infamous events had been discussed within the walls of the four enormous lounge areas and the two equally spacious and elegant dining rooms. Plans had been discussed involving wars, assassinations, investments – in fact most major decisions affecting the lives of each and every one of us had been created, discussed and often chosen by those in power when enjoying the very finest cuisine and a wide range of the world's best and most expensive wines and liquors.

Sir David, taking a sip of the Remy Martin XO cognac just

handed to him, placed the glass on the table at the side of his chair and relaxed back into the soft leather. Sir David Gough, head of MI6, had to now think through the recently created complications surrounding Operation Aries. He was not a man to be ruffled, not easily rushed into making a decision. He'd seen it all before and understood the shortcomings of anyone who'd chosen to invest their lives in a career in the secret service. Sex, money and excitement were the top three most common attractions, and apparently in that order. The revelation made known to him earlier – that it was possible a second operation was in progress to track down the negatives and other material brought back from Iraq by their agent Snowstorm – neither shocked Sir David, nor would it derail his plans. As always he remained totally calm, simply aware of the need to work around the interruptions and retune things. Sir David needed to protect his own very personal interest in Operation Aries. He pondered the possibility of a second operation being in progress. It could be the CIA, or possibly a little nearer to home: Whitehall. Jacqueline Myers, the Home Secretary, would be at the top of Sir David's list. It had even crossed his mind that Peter Astor may have instigated it. But, thought Sir David, that was most unlikely. Peter Astor, whose weakness in resisting the temptations of women and gambling had twice brought him to the edge of personal destruction and bankruptcy. Had it not been for Sir David's ability to negotiate with the media to keep these revelations out of the public domain, not to mention his very generous bailout packages, then Peter Astor's career and family life would have certainly crumbled in the spotlight of scandal and bankruptcy. But Peter was Sir David's closest friend. They'd known each other since Cambridge.

Sir David was one of the Old Guard, a characteristic inherited from his forefathers. His grandfather was a captain in the First World War. He gave his life at the Battle of the Somme while attempting to drag two of his fellow officers to safety who'd been caught by a shower of shrapnel when attempting to cross from one trench to another. And his father, who'd served as a flight commander in the Battle of Britain during the Second World War had an equally impressive record. These characteristics, inherent in Sir David, would not under any circumstances let him see his friend go down.

In the main restaurant Peter Astor had just finished his meal. After pouring back the last few drops of brandy he made his way over to the main lounge.

"Peter, do sit down. How was your meal?"

"Excellent, David. You should have joined me. The lasagne was certainly up to the usual standard."

"I need to talk to you, Peter, about Operation Aries. You are aware of the information we received this morning, I take it?"

Peter Astor, making himself comfortable in the chair next to Sir David, took a perfectly ironed handkerchief out of his pocket and wiped his mouth. Placing this back into his trouser pocket, he looked at Sir David.

"Operation Aries. Yes, I read the reports earlier. All a bit messy if I may say so. Very lucky to have the cooperation of German intelligence. They could quite easily have made things difficult for us. Two bodies and a 7.5 ton truck exploding a couple of hundred yards from a main shopping centre has taken a lot of favours to keep under wraps. And they still have their work cut out keeping our people out of it."

"Yes, but what else do you make of it?"

"Well, the two hired hands are no longer acting for whoever recruited their services, but we are still not in possession of the negatives. These, it would appear from the reports, are still held by Snowstorm. If we're to believe everything in the report, he has now left for Canada. So we need to make contact with him and recommence negotiations."

"Quite right, Peter. I want you to arrange for Catherine McKenzie, who should be arriving at Heathrow airport tomorrow evening, to be met by Special Branch and accompanied to

103

my apartment at River Lodge. We'll need to update her and if necessary, arrange some extra security for her and this Michael McLoughlan fellow until all the competition has died down. Then, as you rightly say, we'll need to restart negotiations with Snowstorm."

"I'll get on to it first thing in the morning David. By the way, what do we know about Michael McLoughlan? Ms McKenzie seems to have managed to recruit his help without much difficulty."

Sir David leant back in his chair. Always relishing the opportunity to demonstrate his ability to memorise all of the most intricate details of any subject he was involved with, he began.

"A thirty-seven-year-old entrepreneur from the Midlands. Has his own small transport business, just secured an order from Les Machines to handle delivery of their machinery for the construction industry for the next twelve months, contract worth around £2 million in gross fees. Divorced some seven years ago, just moved to a place called Birchwood House Farm, Earlswood. Taken out a mortgage in the sum of £465,000. Has an overdraft at Barclays Bank, the limit of which has just been increased to £100,000. Girlfriend's name is Carol Bulman, daughter of Carl Bulman, who died last year leaving his entire estate, including his business, Leeson Holdings, to his two daughters, Carol and Juliet. Total worth according to probate, just over £7 million after taxes. Carol Bulman is now running the business with two co-directors, John Madely and Paul Wright. She lives at the family home, The Beeches, Lapworth, West Midlands."

"Your ability to memorise details never ceases to amaze me, David. But isn't this fellow McLoughlan the same one who picked up the attaché case containing the location details of the negatives Snowstorm was sending over to our embassy in Paris?"

"That's right."

"You don't think he's involved in any way do you? He certainly seems to have got himself right in the middle of everything. First

Paris, now Germany, and according to the reports just received, he's proved himself more than handy with a Gyrojet."

"Well, I certainly hope not. I arranged at Catherine's request a rather sizeable tax refund to help her get this man on board, so to speak. No, I can't see anything there, Peter. The same thought did cross my mind but I don't think he's involved. However, it could be worth checking him out again. Go over things and let me know if you come up with anything which may be of interest. Oh, and by the way, the report from Scotland Yard on that red Toyota hatchback. Apparently it's registered in the name of Graham Carter, one of the gangsters currently working one of the protection rackets in Soho."

"Well, that confirms where the competition recruit their personnel from. All we need to know now is who's doing the recruiting. Is there anything else David?"

"No not at the moment."

Getting up from the chair, Sir David straightened his jacket, finished the last drops of brandy and placed the glass back on the table.

"Now I must go. I need an early night. I have an appointment in the morning with the Prime Minister's undersecretary. Number 10 is doing its usual panicking routine, I'm afraid. Ring me as soon as you have confirmation Ms McKenzie and Mr McLoughlan are successfully on their way back – and make sure Special Branch bring them both straight over to my apartment. We'll take things from there."

Chapter 18

I slept surprisingly well and at just turned 7.30am, I was out of bed, washed and putting on the set of clothes secured for me by Catherine. Not a bad fit, although not exactly my choice. There was a pair of dark grey trousers, a white shirt, and a navy blue blazer. I took a glance in the mirror. The jacket was tight and the trousers about an inch short. At least the shoes fitted. All in all, I couldn't complain. I went into the kitchen. There was coffee, tea, and sugar. When I opened the fridge for the milk, I also noticed sausages, bacon, eggs and two packs of ice cream in the freezer compartment. I made two cups of instant, and returned to the bedroom. I knocked on the door. Catherine was out of bed and dressed in the clothes she'd been supplied with.

"Coffee, Catherine. Sugar's there if you want it."

"You look very smart, Michael. I wondered who it was for a moment."

"Yes alright, let's get all the jokes out of the way. How do you feel anyway, did you sleep alright?"

"Not bad, and thank you for the reassurance of your presence last night, I needed it."

"No problem. I'll see you in a moment."

I put the coffee and sugar bowl on the dressing table and taking my cup, I returned to the lounge. The cottage was small, plainly decorated and sparsely furnished. The lounge had a small settee, an armchair, a bookcase and a small circular table with two rather unsafe looking dining chairs. A mirror on the wall over a tiled fireplace surround gave its age away, thanks to the stains appearing at the corners coming through from the silvered reverse. The curtains looked as though they'd been fitted during the 1960s and, I thought, probably not been disturbed since. The multi-panelled window overlooked a small, but surprisingly tidy rear garden. There was no central heating system; hot water was available from an immersion heater. For everything else there was a two-bar electric fire on the hearth in front of the fireplace, which also looked as if it had been there since the 1960s. This was where we'd be staying for the next twelve to twenty four hours. We wouldn't be able to go out and I was conscious of the fact I needed to get a message to Carol, just to let her know I was alright and with a bit of luck, would be back late Friday or Saturday morning. From all that Catherine had told me it was possible our phone lines at Birchwood House may well be bugged. The only way was to get to a call box. I could telephone Harry at the Crown Inn and ask him to drive over to Birchwood House Farm and let Carol know I was alright. It would take a bit of explaining but I couldn't think of any other way.

Catherine came into the lounge with a pack of playing cards, a pad and a pencil.

"I hope you're into playing cards, Michael."

"I am as it happens, but I must warn you, I cheat."

"So do I."

Catherine pulled up the small coffee table at the side of the settee. Sitting opposite me, she dealt out the cards.

We played pontoon, poker, three card brag, snap and an assortment of impromptu variations of the same games. We ate eggs and bacon for lunch, the same for tea and sandwiches for supper. By one o'clock Friday morning Catherine was indebted to me to the sum of £765,000.

"Right, Michael. Double or quits, then I'm off to bed."

Catherine won – we were back to square one. We went to bed and both slept until 8am the following morning.

After finishing off the remaining eggs and bacon for breakfast I was keen to get moving. I hoped the arrangements for our new passports and flight back to England wouldn't take much longer. Catherine, reading the text message she'd just received, confirmed my wish had been granted.

"Just received a text, Michael. Our escort will be here in about half an hour."

It was precisely half an hour, almost to the minute, when a middle-aged couple driving a somewhat scruffy looking dark blue Audi saloon pulled up outside the cottage.

After a brief introduction we got into the car and began the drive to the airport. I sat in the front, Catherine in the rear. The man driving was about 45 years of age. He wore a cream sweater and a pair of dark grey trousers not dissimilar to the ones I'd been given but not, I thought, from his wardrobe. The guy was some six inches shorter than me and I reckoned a good two stones heavier. He introduced himself as Edgar, and his wife, sitting next to Catherine, was called Eva. A few minutes into our journey Edgar began the conversation.

"We're here to help you both get back to England, Michael. We have new passports and identity papers plus two tickets for your flight to Heathrow London which is scheduled to take off at 7pm this evening from Frankfurt Airport."

"Are you both with the embassy?"

My question was ignored. Catherine saved me from the silence.

"My companion is not with our security services."

"Well, Michael, my wife Eva and I are here to assist you and Catherine to get back to London safely. We're driving now to Frankfurt Airport. In the glove compartment there are your passports and some papers. You and Catherine look through them and familiarise yourselves with your new temporary identities.

We have about a forty-minute drive before we reach the airport so you'll need to memorise all the information by then. There are two cases in the boot with your names and flight details. They've been packed with the usual assortment of clothes and accessories anyone would be expected to take for a two-day break. You are both lecturers at the University of Westminster and are returning from a two-day conference you've attended on public speaking and oral interaction at Cullene University, Hamburg. The seminar was headed by Professor Shineman. You, Michael, are single, divorced and living in Westminster at the address detailed on the notes I've written down for you. You, Catherine, are married and living in Ealing with your husband and two children. Your husband is currently looking after the children while you're away. You have both attended the conference with three other associates. You'll see their details on the same list of notes I've made for you. You are both now returning to England a day earlier than your associates. You, Catherine, to get back to your family, and you, Michael, to get back to prepare papers for an examination your students are preparing to take next week. Michael, you teach mechanical engineering and, Catherine, you are a lecturer in media studies.

I began to look through the notes that I assumed had been made by Edgar and his wife and wondered if all this was really necessary. Like anyone passing through customs, we might have our baggage checked, but surely not questioned as we seemed to be preparing for.

"You're thinking all this is perhaps unnecessary, yes?"

"Well, it was crossing my mind, Edgar."

Edgar looked in the driving mirror at Catherine.

"You're right, Catherine, Michael doesn't work for SIS. He's obviously not used to all this cloak and dagger business."

Catherine smiled.

"Don't worry, Michael. It's just a precaution. We just need to be sure we've covered every possible contingency."

Eva turned to Catherine.

"You'd better let me have the pistols now, Catherine, and anything else you're carrying. And Michael, do you have anything we need to take from you before we reach the airport?"

"Not that I'm aware of. All my papers, my driving licence, my passport, along with everything else, went up with the truck."

Turning round I saw Catherine hand over the two pistols and a couple of small boxes I assumed to be ammunition.

"Just the mobiles now then. We'll be at the airport in a few minutes. It's only about a mile further on, past the next set of traffic lights."

We pulled up outside the departures entrance to Frankfurt Airport. I shook hands with Edgar and his wife Eva and thanked them for their assistance. I got our cases from the boot of the car. Then Catherine and I walked through the enormous automatic glass doors and made our way to the departures counter.

After checking in we had over an hour before we would be called to board our plane. We made our way up the escalator to the first floor and walked past all the shops and over towards the departure lounge. I got us two coffees and a magazine for Catherine. I then decided to take the opportunity of getting a message through to Carol. I was aware from what Catherine had told me it was possible the phones both at Carol's house and Birchwood House Farm could be bugged, but I had my plan. I went over to one of the phone booths with a handful of euros and dialled the Crown Inn.

"Harry, it's me, Michael. I want you to do a favour for me. Can you go over to Carol's place: The Beeches, Stratford Road, Lapworth, and give her a message for me? Tell her I've had a problem with the truck but I'll be back sometime tomorrow, probably tomorrow evening. Harry, I can't explain now but don't whatever you do telephone her. Go over and give her the message personally. Will you do that for me?"

"The Beeches, Michael? That bloody big place a couple of miles before you get to Henley in Arden?"

"That's the one, Harry, and listen, whatever you do don't telephone her – go over in person."

"Alright Michael, whatever you say. By the way, this hasn't got anything to do with that woman who left the note for you the other evening has it?"

"Harry, it's got everything to do with her, but it's not what you're thinking. I'll tell you all about it when I get back."

"Don't worry. I've been in more scrapes over the years than you've had speeding tickets. I'll go over now, before we get busy."

"Thanks Harry, I owe you one."

I returned to our table. Catherine had finished browsing through the magazine I'd bought her.

"You've got your new identity all clearly in your mind, Michael?"

"I have. I think I have anyway. Tell you what..." Taking out of my jacket pocket the list I'd been given, I handed it to Catherine. "You ask away, then it's my turn."

Our question and answer routine whiled away a good forty minutes or so, by which time the call to board our plane came over the PA system.

Our flight was completely uneventful, as was the check out at customs. There was absolutely no need for the new identity routine, but I resisted making the point to Catherine.

We arrived at Heathrow at 9.50pm and again, absolutely no delay through customs. Making our way across to the arrivals exit, we were greeted by two guys I assumed to be from our security services.

"Good evening, Catherine and good evening, Michael. Would you follow us please?"

I looked at Catherine, who obviously knew the men escorting us and had no doubt been expecting them.

"Our car is just over here. We have a short drive."

"A short drive to where?" I asked the guy opening the door for me.

Catherine answered for him.

"We need to go through a debriefing interview. Perfectly normal, it shouldn't take very long."

Chapter 19

Nothing much changes, I thought, listening to the rain pounding the roof and windows of our chauffeur driven Jaguar as we headed towards our debriefing interview – as Catherine had described it. I began to wonder what exactly that entailed and whether Harry had managed to get my message to Carol. Thirty minutes into our journey I decided to ask another question – maybe this time I'd get an answer. Turning to the driver, I asked where we were heading.

"River Lodge Apartments, Grosvenor Road. About another fifteen minutes and we'll be there."

"Sir David's apartment then?" enquired Catherine. "Will he be there, or Peter Astor, do you know?"

"No idea I'm afraid. I just have instructions to pick you both up from Heathrow and take you there."

"Anything new been happening while I was away or don't you know?"

"Sorry, Catherine, you know what it's like! Haven't been told a thing apart from hearing Sir David had an appointment at Number 10 this morning. There's certainly some excitement going on over something or other, but I've no idea what."

We pulled up outside River Lodge Apartments. Catherine and I walked through the canopied entrance and into the main hallway, which was impressive to say the least. I remembered seeing a programme a few months back on apartments overlooking the Thames. I wasn't sure whether the documentary used this location but what I did remember was the prices these places went for. Around £3 million for a one-bedroom, ground floor plot, to over £5 million for a three-bedroom, top floor plot.

As we walked across the marble tiled floor I was trying to imagine spending all those millions for an apartment. The escalator, silently taking us to the eighth floor, gave the feeling of being escorted in a gold-plated carriage. We exited our 'carriage of gold' and stepped into Sir David's apartment. The hallway was enormous and seemed to disappear along metres of marble flooring. A wall of glass with two sliding glass doors framed the magical view of Westminster and the River Thames. The balcony furnished with several tables and chairs, all set to provide a place to relax and enjoy this unbelievable view. I was beginning to understand the several-million-pounds price tag for all this. One of our escorts turned to me.

"Michael, you wait here. Sir David will want to speak with Catherine first."

I continued to look out over the Thames and the thousands of lights illuminating the city, like a galaxy from another world. Then I heard the unmistakable sound of Big Ben, as he stamped his authority on the scene.

Some twenty minutes later the door to the lounge opened and Catherine beckoned to me.

"Pretty well all completed now, Michael, but Sir David would like to meet you."

We walked into the lounge. Sir David Gough walked over and shook my hand.

"Michael, Catherine has told me all about the help you've given her these past few days and I'd like to add my gratitude for your assistance here. Now, I'm sure you'll understand that nothing of what you've been involved in must be conveyed to anyone. Forgive me for making this point. I know you'll understand the importance of total secrecy and I know we'll be able to rely on your discretion. The German authorities have given us their assurance that their police will be making no further investigations into the events of the past couple of days, at least as far as you're concerned. The incident regarding the destruction of your vehicle will be officially recorded as an accident caused by a petrol leak from one of the vehicles parked close by. You'll have no problems with either your insurance claim or transport regulators. I'll make sure of that. Now, as a precaution, I'm arranging for a couple of our officers from Special Branch to keep an eye on things for you when you get back to the Midlands. They'll keep out of the way. You won't even know they're there, but you can relax and get on with the day-to-day running of your business in the knowledge we will be looking after everything from now on." Picking up a folder of papers, Sir David placed them on the coffee table. "Michael, I need you to sign a copy of the Official Secrets Act with regards to this matter. You are an intelligent man and I know you'll understand the importance of keeping the events of the last few days absolutely secret."

Handing me a pen, Sir David pointed to where he wished me to sign. I signed and dated the document then placed the pen on the coffee table.

Sir David got up from his chair and turned to me.

"I think that concludes everything. Again, many thanks. Your assistance in this matter has helped our intelligence services and we are all extremely grateful."

As I stood up and shook hands again with Sir David I noticed something among the papers on the coffee table which somehow looked familiar – a logo on top of a letter protruding from one of the folders. It seemed to touch a memory cell somewhere. Where had I seen it before? I was tired and anxious to get back to Birchwood House Farm so any further exploration of my thoughts would have to wait – for the moment anyway.

"Can one of your officers drop me at Paddington Station? I can get a train from there to Birmingham."

"No need for that, Michael, one of our officers will drive you back home."

I came out of the lounge into the enormous hallway. Catherine followed me and took hold of my hand.

"Michael, thanks for everything. I'll be in touch."

I wished her well and asked her to let me know how Georgina got on with her treatment in America. Then I again suggested, in a low voice, that she should perhaps concentrate on journalism rather than all this bullet dodging. Turning round I entered the gold-plated carriage of the elevator and in almost complete silence, descended to the ground floor and back into the reception of River Lodge Apartments. One of the officers chatting to the concierge looked up.

"Michael, ready for the drive back home?"

Perhaps now, I thought, I can get back to running my business and get on with the plans I'd started for our expansion programme.

"Ready when you are."

116

Chapter 20

The XF certainly lived up to all the reports I'd read on this latest creation from Jaguar. Powerful, smooth running, very comfortable and handled expertly by my appointed chauffeur.

"They hand these sort of cars out at MI6 do they Graham?"

"I'm actually with Special Branch, Michael. I prefer to spend my weekends at home with my wife and family. Spent six years at the Met, then took the opportunity of moving over to Special Branch a couple of years ago."

"Are you enjoying the work?"

"It's not bad. A lot of the time is spent going over the same boring routine but now and again, we get called on to do something interesting."

Graham made a good travelling companion and certainly knew how to handle the new Jaguar. He also joined me in a cigarette as we turned onto the M1. Then we really began to motor. I still preferred my XK150 but this new creation from Jaguar was good. Very good in fact.

The journey back to the Midlands took under two hours. It had just turned 2.45am when Graham dropped me at Birchwood House Farm. I walked through into the hallway and wondered if Carol might have sorted the bedroom out. For the life of me I couldn't remember how things had been left. As I walked across the hallway

I thought to myself that this was the very first opportunity I'd had to have an uninterrupted look around the place I'd virtually signed my life away for just over a week ago. Then I heard a door opening upstairs followed by the landing light switching on. It was Carol.

"Michael! You're back at last!"

Carol came running down the stairs in the shortest of nightdresses and put her arms around me.

"Got your message from Harry, but what on earth has been happening?"

Just like my exploration of Birchwood House Farm, the explanations, I thought, can wait till morning. Carol and I retired to the bedroom and remained there.

I woke at 7.45am, showered, dressed and went downstairs to the kitchen.

"Made us some breakfast, Michael. Come on, bring it out onto the patio, let's eat out there."

It had only just turned 8am but the sky was clear and the sun was beginning to flex its muscles. We sat at the patio table and I ploughed through the eggs and bacon Carol had made. It was good, and certainly needed. The last really decent meal I'd had in over four days was the meal Carol had made last Monday evening.

"So come on, what's been happening? Harry said you'd had some problems with the truck breaking down or something, but why didn't you telephone me?"

I was not convinced Operation Aries was safe to talk about. I had, just a few hours ago, signed the official secrets document at the request of Sir David Gough, the head of MI6, no less. Apart from that, if the revelations made to me by Catherine were accurate, and weapons of mass destruction had in fact been supplied to Iraq prior to the invasion by this country and the US, then this was literally a ticking bomb just waiting to go off. However, I knew Carol by now. If there was one person on this planet I could trust, it was her. She was by no means the usual stay-at-home wife, which was probably one of her main attractions for me.

"There's quite a bit to tell you and a lot to get your head around." I lit one of my Marlboro cigarettes and took another swig of coffee.

Carol looked at me and smiled.

"Come on then, let's have it."

"When I was in Paris I was nearly knocked down by a car which mounted the pavement behind me as I was walking back to my hotel. The car had been stolen and was being pursued by the local police. I didn't mention the incident because I didn't want you worrying about something that at the time seemed of little importance. Anyway, the kids who'd stolen the car were chucking out everything they thought of no value – including an attaché case which landed on the pavement in front of me. I picked it up and took it back with me to the hotel. I thought no more about it. When I got back home, as you are well aware, we were far too busy with more important things than for me to go on about an incident I believed was of no consequence. Anyway, one of the correspondents working for the BBC, Catherine McKenzie, contacted me. She told me that in the attaché case was a letter addressed to the British Embassy in Paris. Apparently the letter gave details of the location of some photographs which had been taken in Iraq prior to the invasion, showing ballistic missiles being assembled at two locations in Baghdad. Catherine McKenzie not only works for the BBC, but from time to time gets involved with investigative work for MI6. She asked me to take her to Hamburg when making the delivery of that equipment for Les Machines. She was attempting to make contact with the MI6 agent in Germany who'd apparently found the photographs along with a load of other documents, including letters between our government, Saddam Hussein and Colonel Gaddafi, which could turn out to be very embarrassing to say the least. This agent of theirs was apparently blackmailing our government for the return of all these documents. Catherine believed, because of the nature of the investigation she was handling, that she was more than likely being shadowed by one or more interested parties. So, as a consequence, she wanted to make the journey to Germany under an alias."

I decided to water down the remaining events in Germany, and simplified the story.

"My truck developed problems – fuel pump, I think. Anyway some people working for SIS over there arranged a flight back home for us. I was asked not to take my mobile as it was possible it could have been tagged, hence my arrangement for Harry to get a message through to you."

I felt better that Carol knew the gist of what I'd become involved in, but I was also aware of the very serious and possibly dangerous implications.

Carol looked concerned at the revelations I'd just made but appreciated being brought into the picture.

"So what happens now, Michael? Do you think it might be an idea to get some advice? Maybe from someone who knows how our secret service operates?"

"I already met the head of MI6 in London last night before making the journey back here. There's nowhere else I can get advice from. Not as far as I know anyway. He gave me the impression everything was under control, so at the moment there really is very little more I can do. He gave me his assurance that they would be handling things from here on in and there was absolutely need for me to concern myself anymore.

Anyway, changing the subject, how do you fancy staying here for a few days and helping to organise things? What with you and Theresa, we'll have this place running like clockwork before you know it."

"Theresa and I had already decided on that, Michael. I've got a good team handling things at Leeson Holdings so I can help out here for a while, no problem. You just concentrate on keeping out of trouble and bringing in the business. We'll take care of everything else."

"That's a deal then, Carol?"

Theresa and her new assistants were busy going through all the paperwork in the office. The new timetable for Saturday was 9am to 5.30pm. Gordon was also busy working on two of the trucks for Monday. A delivery had been booked to collect three more machines from the Les Machines factory in Liverpool and get them back here ready for delivery on Tuesday to contractors working just outside Southampton.

This morning I needed to go through the quotes for converting the barns into holiday cottages and then next week I'd organise getting that project underway. I knew Gary was short of work at present so I reckoned he could start as soon as I gave him the go ahead. The day literally flew past. I'd asked Carol to invite Theresa and her husband to join us for a curry at the Rajnagar restaurant that evening. They enthusiastically agreed and I booked the table for 8.30pm.

Chapter 21

I decided to spend Sunday going over the plans for updating and decorating Birchwood House Farm. I was, however, more interested in getting the holiday cottages finished before spending very much on the main house. I could make do with everything as it was for a while. In my opinion, an updated kitchen or new bathroom suite came a poor second to the rental income which could be generated by letting out the cottages. Carol, however, was rather more interested in updating Birchwood House so the decision was made to get both projects underway at the same time. There could be some benefit, I thought. Maybe some savings could be made on labour and material costs doing it this way. I certainly hoped so.

The next week was like something out of War and Peace. Gary and his team of contractors took over updating the electrics I knew were required at the house, and his plumbing contractors, having ripped out both the bathroom and kitchen, were busy laying the new system. The same at the barns: electrics were updated there and a new plumbing system installed. All meals were takeaways and I made use of the bathroom at Carol's house, which was very conveniently only a fifteen-minute drive away. I'd decided not to leave the property unattended at night until the new alarm system and security lights had been fitted.

After another week, the kitchen and bathroom at Birchwood

House, although far from finished, were at least usable. The barns had also made good progress. I reckoned it would take another couple of weeks or so to decorate and finish before we'd be home and dry. The driveway to the cottages needed updating and would, I hoped, soon be used by the tenants I was banking on. The drainage system would need improving and either a new layer of pebbles or re-tarmacking would be required. That job though, could certainly wait until next year. All in all, things were taking shape and I had resigned myself to the fact I would be holding a paintbrush in my hand for the next few weeks, painting anything that looked remotely unfinished.

Carol had now returned to her role as Managing Director of Leeson Holdings but came back most evenings and was beginning to get used to the new kitchen but not, the rather uncomfortable double bed, which I promised we'd exchange for a new model at the weekend.

The office was busy. Theresa and her new recruits were working flat out. Two new contracts had been received from a subsidiary of Les Machines and we would need the addition of two further trucks on top of the seven I'd already arranged to lease. Next month, five additional drivers would be joining our team. The recruitment agency had also managed to find a new mechanic to assist Gordon with all the servicing and repairs. Theresa had streamlined our filing system, putting most of the mountains of paperwork on two new computers we had installed. Everyone had been working like hell and our efforts were slowly being rewarded. From the dust I could see the emergence of MCL Carriers and Birchwood House Farm. It was a good feeling.

It had just turned 10.30pm when I decided to call it a day at the office. I walked across the hallway to the lounge, poured myself a large glass of wine and for the first time in weeks, I switched on the television and relaxed in the armchair by the fireplace. The programme running was Newsnight – all the usual doom and gloom about the world's economy. The problems with the government's strategy to combat the problems were being eloquently conveyed by members of the opposition invited to make their comments. Then came a report on the Prime Minister's visit to Afghanistan earlier in the day to meet with the troops and confirm the country's indebtedness to their continuing efforts and bravery. The report was compiled and broadcast by Catherine McKenzie. It was good to see her in the role of correspondent and I hoped she'd taken my advice and given up any further involvement with our security services. Then, just after the national weather forecast, came a breaking news report: The BBC war correspondent, Catherine McKenzie, and two members of the BBC film crew, had reportedly been killed when their truck drove over a land mine somewhere in Helmand Province. They had been returning after reporting on the Prime Minister's visit to the area earlier that day.

Chapter 22

The news hit me deep in the pit of my stomach. She was a lovely woman. Why the hell did she continue risking her life – not only reporting from the most dangerous places around the world but also getting herself involved in the murky waters of our secret service? I felt the loss of someone I believed could have been a good friend. She was one of those rare people you meet occasionally and connect with straight away. I wondered how Georgina would handle things. Catherine had mentioned they'd been together for some years. I wondered, had she accompanied Catherine to Afghanistan? She did tell me she helped from time to time with her journalism work. And what about the operation and treatment Georgina needed? Would that still go ahead? All these thoughts and a sense of loss were running through me. But most of all, there was an overriding anger and frustration at not being able to do anything. I would try to get in touch with Georgina. The only way I could think of was to make contact with the BBC. I'd no idea of Catherine's home address. Georgina had told me they lived somewhere in Worcester. I decided I'd give it a few days before making any enquiries.

I had a lousy night's sleep. All the feelings of sadness and frustration at what had happened were still very much with me the following morning. After breakfast I went into the office to go over the accounts for the previous week. Theresa and our two new assistants were there working away, returning all the calls received overnight and planning the routes for our drivers. After finishing the accounts and completing the list of expenses for all the refurbishments, I made out a cheque to A. R. Smith, one of the builder's merchants, and one for ABS Machine Hire for the heaters we'd used to speed up drying the plasterwork in the barns. All ready now, I thought, for my handiwork with the paintbrush. Still feeling the need to occupy my thoughts to avoid dwelling on yesterday's news, I decided I would make a start on the decorating that afternoon.

I left Theresa, Louise and Melissa to continue with all the paperwork and telephone calls and wandered into the kitchen. I made a coffee, lit a cigarette and sat outside on the patio looking over the two and a half acres of gardens stretching down from Birchwood House to the barns. They would soon, I thought, be two holiday cottages ready for letting. I looked over to the barn on the right of the property which we'd converted into the service garage and just beyond that, the paddock used for parking the trucks. All ready to start up again tomorrow and to continue turning the wheels of our expansion programme and the creation of the new enterprise we'd set in motion.

I had to think positively now and put the events of the last couple of weeks to the back of my mind, along with the news of Catherine's untimely death. I was still unable to stop asking myself whether I could have done anything to prevent it. When I'd talked with Catherine about giving up her work with our secret services, could I have been more positive? Could I have said anything else which may have altered the chain of events? I reminded myself she was killed when carrying out her work as correspondent, not during some operation for MI6. Or at least that's how it seemed. But all that didn't help much. I still felt in some way I'd let her down. Unrealistic I know, but that's how I felt.

I finished my coffee and cigarette and made my way back to

the office. I remembered I needed to send an email to the builder's merchant to order a list of materials to finish the drainage at the barns: guttering, downpipes and another load of sand and gravel for the outside walkway we were putting there.

I went back to the office and switched on the computer. It was one of the new ones Theresa had set up. Not having used it before, and with my very limited knowledge of the workings of computers, I was unable to get into the programme I needed. Theresa and the girls were taking their lunch break. Not wanting to risk messing up the new system, I closed it down and went over to my computer. I clicked in and went into the Hotmail system. There, in the inbox was a message. A sudden and very strange feeling came over me as I read the introduction.

CatherineMcKenzie@Codemail.com has sent you a
Secure email. To read it please visit the following web page.

A web link was listed. I clicked and was immediately transferred to a website for an email encryption service.

Your message has been protected. You must answer the following question to retrieve this. You are limited to three incorrect answers.

Question: The name of your University?

The name of the university given to us by Edgar and Eva, I thought. I typed in my answer: Westminster.

Fast moving developments, Michael. Please can you meet
George, same place as last time. 11am Monday 30th June.
BE VERY CAREFUL. DON'T TRUST ANYONE.
Catherine

The message had been sent two days ago. Georgina would probably not turn up now, but I had to go, just in case. And what the hell was the warning in capital letters all about: BE VERY CAREFUL. DON'T TRUST ANYONE. Was it possible Catherine's death in Afghanistan was connected to Operation Aries?

I closed down the computer and on getting up from the desk, I noticed some papers sent to us by Martin McGovern suggesting ideas for the new business logo. Something there seemed to catch my attention. I began looking through the ideas Martin had sent us. All the suggestions he'd made consisted of a simple row of letters in bright red:

MCL

Carriers

There were several alternative designs suggesting a different layout for the initials MCL but all with the same idea of a simple design which would be easily remembered. It was this that reminded me of the logo I'd seen at Sir David's apartment, on a compliments slip or letterhead which had been protruding out of one of the files on the coffee table. Then I remembered where I'd seen the same logo before: on the piece of torn envelope Heidi had used to write the message to her landlord confirming she'd left the keys to her apartment at the Alder Coffee House. Something at the back of my mind was attempting to make sense.

What were the initials on that envelope? B O A R. I typed them into Google. The list appeared: Boardmasters, Boardman Bikes, Boardman Empire, Board Games, Board. None of those.

I tried B A O R. The list appeared: British and American Oil Refineries. I went into the first on the list: 'British and American Oil Refineries. Refineries in Libya and Iraq. Oil exploration and production, including petrochemical complex, including ethylene and polythene plants. Current production: 220,000 barrels per day. A simple hydroskimming refining process.'

All of the details meant little to me except that when I compared the current production of 220,000 barrels per day to other refineries listed, it was obvious this company's production was big – and according to the information given there were plans to build a further two refinery plants in 2012.

Chapter 23

I parked in the multi-storey car park at Touchwood shopping centre. It had just turned 10.15am. I had no idea whether Georgina would turn up for the meeting Catherine had emailed me about, but I was determined to be there. I was now hell-bent on finding and uncovering all I could about Operation Aries and Catherine's sudden death in Afghanistan. Was there a connection? I really had no idea. Common sense told me I was out of my depth in all this, but I wasn't about to give up. Somehow I would find the answers. I just felt I had no alternative.

A couple of weeks ago it had seemed like a bombshell of a discovery that the West had probably been supplying ballistic missiles to the Saddam regime. Now it seemed to be taking an even more sinister twist. Catherine's warning to be careful and not to trust anyone was beginning to make more sense.

I descended the escalator from the car park into the shopping mall. There was a fair number of people about – not overly busy, but this was Monday morning. Come Saturday, you'd need to fight your way through. I walked past the parade of shops to the entrance of the John Lewis department store and took the escalator to the electrical department where I'd first met Georgina a couple of weeks previously.

I was early. Another twenty minutes, I thought, and if Georgina was going to keep the appointment she'd be here by then. I walked around the department, looking at all the latest widescreen televisions, iPods and Kindles. I walked past the chandeliers and the many different desk lamps and wall lights, none of which I was really taking much notice of. My mind was focused on one thing and one thing only. Would Georgina keep the appointment? I looked over to the other side of the store and had my answer – Georgina was descending the escalator. I walked over to meet her. She looked pale. She was smartly dressed just as the first time we'd met, but there had been less attention to detail. Her hair was brushed back and held tightly at the back of her head by two odd hair grips. Some strands of hair left loose dropped over her cheeks. Her eyes looked sore and her make-up looked somewhat patchy, as if hurriedly applied without much thought. I took her hand.

"Georgina. I'm so very sorry."

I couldn't think of anything else to say. A feeling of hopelessness came over me as I looked into her empty eyes. The life had been dragged out of her. She looked almost vacant, past caring.

"Georgina, let me get you a coffee or something."

"Okay, but not here, Michael. I'd prefer to be outside. Anywhere in the open air."

"Not a problem. Come on, let's walk outside."

We strolled back through the shopping mall and out into the high street. In silence we walked down the high street into Mell Square. Georgina sat at one of the tables outside the Costa coffee house while I got us a couple of cappuccinos. We both lit a cigarette and sipped our coffees. Georgina broke the silence.

"Catherine wanted to get in touch with you, Michael. She was genuinely concerned for your safety as well as ours. Operation Aries, she told me, was becoming more and more complicated by the day and she was worried about the implications of what she was beginning to piece together."

"Did she tell you anything? Anything about what she was working on, what was worrying her?"

"No, she always did keep details of any work involving our security services to herself. She rarely spoke about ~~her~~ the work, except with this bloody Aries operation she was involved with. She did tell me before flying out to Afghanistan to cover the Prime Minister's visit that if anything should happen to her I was to contact you and warn you to be careful. She'd made some notes which you might be able to make some sense of."

From a large handbag, Georgina handed me an A5 sized diary with a ring folder section for notes. It reminded me of the Filofax diaries everyone used to carry around with them back in the late 1980s.

"Catherine believed the only way to get rid of any threat created by the operation she'd been working on was to make the revelations public. The problem with that, she told me, was the revelations were too big and too far reaching to be believed. The threat to anyone with knowledge of what she believed had been happening ~~would remain~~ could be fatal. Catherine, as I've already told you, didn't discuss her work with me, but she'd made some notes here. She told me as soon as she'd returned from Afghanistan she was going to make contact with you and asked me to send an email to arrange this meeting." Georgina opened the diary and handed it to me. "These are some of the notes Catherine had been making. This one, a cryptic note she'd made just before flying out to Afghanistan, she believed was probably the final piece of the jigsaw. The key to Operation Aries, as she put it. I've no idea what it means but Catherine was convinced it held the answers she'd been looking for."

The bad weather is now over.
Everyone loves Mozart.
857753770

"Now I must go. I'm staying with some friends in Portsmouth and my train leaves in thirty minutes."

"Do you have a contact number, Georgina? I'd like to have the opportunity of keeping in touch with you, if I may?"

Georgina looked thoughtful, then with a forced smile, looked at me. Was it possible she blamed me in any way for what had happened to Catherine or did she just want to get as far away as possible from anything or anyone who reminded her of the past few days?

"I will ring you, Michael, one day. Good luck with everything."

We shook hands. Georgina walked across the square towards the train station.

I got myself another cappuccino, lit a cigarette and began staring at yet another cryptic message which may or may not lead me to the answers I was looking for. I reminded myself I didn't even know the questions I needed answers to. It did cross my mind to destroy the diary, forget the whole thing and get on with building my business and looking after things at Birchwood House Farm. However, I knew myself well enough to know that wasn't going to happen. I needed to think things through and try to decipher the message in Catherine's diary – not that I was much good on the first attempt, trying to work out that coded message giving the location details of where Snowstorm had apparently hidden the photographs and all the papers he'd found in Iraq. I stared at the cryptic message Catherine had written in her diary: 'The bad weather is over.' Could that refer to Snowstorm, the MI6 agent we unsuccessfully attempted to track down in Germany? Had he disappeared somewhere or been assassinated? The message seemed to suggest he was gone. If I was thinking along the right lines, that is. And 'Everyone loves Mozart'? What on earth did that mean? Music? Concerts? Or had it something to do with an address in Vienna? Was it possible that Heidi or someone connected to Operation Aries was living in Vienna? Even if my thinking was anywhere near correct it didn't really help at all. How the hell was I going to track down someone who may or may not live somewhere in Vienna, and someone who may or may not have any knowledge of Operation Aries? It did cross my mind to make contact with Sir David Gough but I was convinced that was not the way forward.

I began to flick through the list of names and telephone numbers at the front of Catherine's diary. Maybe if I could make contact with one of Catherine's colleagues, possibly even someone who had been working with her in Iraq, it may help. I went down the list of names. Two seemed more probable than the others. First, there was Peter Ripley, editor of Newsnight. Surely he'd be able to refer me to associates who had knowledge of Catherine's work? That's if he'd be willing to speak with me and reveal that information. A little further down the list was the name John Williams, war correspondent for The Telegraph. It was possible that he may have been reporting in Iraq at the time Catherine was out there.

I knew I had to be cautious – something which I was becoming more and more aware of. I couldn't just go around revealing all that I'd learnt from Catherine about Snowstorm and everything that had happened in Germany. It was obvious my knowledge of the investigation Catherine had been working on put my life in very real danger. For the first time since that bloody car in Paris almost ploughed me into the pavement of Rue du Faubourg Saint-Honoré, I not only felt the danger but realised I was very much on my own.

Chapter 24

Remembering Catherine had warned me our phones may have been hacked, I got myself some loose change by buying twenty cigarettes, then walked over to one of the few remaining phone boxes on Warwick Road. I dialled the number for Peter Ripley, editor of Newsnight. I was eventually put through to his office.

"Can I help you?"

The woman's voice was sharp and businesslike. Still aware of the need for caution, I decided to use an alias.

"My name is James Murray. Can you put me through to Peter Ripley?"

"He's tied up at the moment. What is it you need to speak to Mr Ripley about? Or can I help you?"

"I have information relating to an investigation Catherine McKenzie was working on and would like to discuss this with Mr Ripley."

"What did you say your name was?"

"James Murray."

"If you leave me your number, Mr Murray, I'll get someone to call you back."

"Forgive me but what I need to speak to Mr Ripley about is both confidential and very urgent. I need to speak with him or at least someone who's familiar with Catherine's work."

I held the line, as requested, for what seemed like hours. The sharp, businesslike voice returned.

"Mr Murray, if you wish to call here tomorrow and ask for me at reception, Barbara Littleton, I'll see if I can arrange a meeting for you. But I'm not promising anything. Mr Ripley is extremely busy at the moment as I'm sure you'll appreciate, following the death of Ms McKenzie last week. However, if you wish to call at the main reception area at Portland Place I'll see what I can do."

I thanked the sharp, businesslike voice, which now had a name – Barbara Littleton. I said I'd be there tomorrow morning around 9am.

Opening Catherine's diary I dialled the number for John Williams. The number was a landline. I'd no idea whether it was his office or home number, but it was the only number Catherine had listed for him.

"Four seven eight three."

The voice was slurred. I thought maybe I'd just woken him up or I'd got the wrong number.

"Mr Williams...is that John Williams?"

"It is. Who's calling?"

"Mr Williams, we haven't spoken before. My name is James Murray. I got your number from Catherine McKenzie. I wondered if I might call to see you. I need some advice. A couple of weeks ago I became involved in an investigation Catherine was working on. As you've probably heard, Catherine was killed the other day when reporting in Afghanistan and I'm trying to tie up some loose ends."

The line was silent.

"Mr Williams...are you still there?"

"What did you say your name was?"

"James Murray. Can I call to see you tomorrow? It really is very important."

There was a long pause.

"Where are you calling from, Mr Murray?"

"I'm in the Midlands. I have an appointment with Peter Ripley at the BBC tomorrow morning to see if he can help and I wondered if I could call round to see you after then?"

"I don't know who you are Mr Murray, but if you really want to talk with me then I suggest you get here before midday. I open my first bottle at 12.30 and quite frankly old boy, everything goes downhill from then on."

This guy was seriously drunk. That was obvious. But I thought he may just be the one with some answers.

"Mr Williams, thank you. I'll call you tomorrow."

Chapter 25

The following morning I left a note for Theresa saying I was on appointments all day but would telephone her later. I caught the 6.30am train from New Street Station which arrived at Paddington at 8.10. A taxi ride later, I arrived at Broadcasting House.

The enormous reception hall at BBC headquarters was busy. I gave my name to the receptionist who said she'd contact Barbara Littleton and let her know I'd arrived.

I took a seat and glanced briefly through a couple of magazines on the chair next to me. After about thirty minutes I walked back to the reception desk and waited patiently in the queue for my chance to enquire whether Miss Littleton would be much longer. I heard someone behind me insisting he was not James Murray. I turned round and saw a man about my age and height who'd sat where I'd been sitting. He was arguing with two men. Unless I was much mistaken, he was about to be arrested.

I walked back from the reception area over to the toilets. I went in and waited. I was aware of the sensitivity of what I'd become involved in regarding Catherine's investigation, but the arrest of that poor sod a few moments ago brought it home to me. That's the second time someone else had unwittingly been mistaken for me, I thought. First Paris, and now here in London.

I had to move fast. God knows if my luck would hold out long enough for me to get the answers I needed. Then I reminded myself that I wasn't even sure of the questions I needed answers to. My mind was on autopilot. Somehow, from somewhere, I needed to get some sense out of someone. There were guys coming in and out of the toilets. I walked over to the wash basins, washed my hands and dried them under the drier while continuing to think things through. One thing was for sure, I needed to get away before the police, Special Branch officers or whoever they were, realised they'd arrested the wrong man. I walked out of the toilets, across the reception hall and out of Broadcasting House. I walked down Portland Place and continued walking until I came to a public phone box. I dialled the number for John Williams.

"Mr Williams, it's James Murray. We spoke briefly yesterday – is it convenient for me to call to see you?"

"Mr Murray, I hope you are not wasting my time, but yes, I can give you five minutes. My address is 47 Victoria Avenue, North Finchley, just off Woodhouse Road."

A tube journey and taxi ride later, I arrived at number 47 Victoria Avenue.

Chapter 26

I rang the bell to number 47, a large three-storey Victorian residence. A rather attractive, fifty-something woman, opened the door.

"I have an appointment with Mr Williams. My name is James Murray."

"Yes Mr Murray, my husband is expecting you. Follow me would you?"

Closing the door behind me, I followed Mrs Williams down the hallway and through a door into the rear reception room. This was obviously the study. However, it looked more like one of the store cupboards at Waterstones. At the far end of the room, in front of the patio doors, there was a desk with a computer, an abundance of papers piling over the edges of several wire-framed trays, and two glasses with two bottles of wine, unopened. There were two easy chairs and what must have been over a thousand books, reference files and folders of all sizes piled up on the floor. A tall, slightly plump gentleman entered the room wearing light cream jeans, a white cheesecloth shirt and beige carpet slippers. He looked about what I'd expected. Mid-sixties, capable, a no nonsense sort of character, but unless I was mistaken, the booze was beginning to beat him. His eyes were bright blue but black-bagged underneath. He was ruddy around the cheeks and nose.

"Right, Mr Murray, fire away. How can I help you?"

"I'm not altogether sure. I'm looking for advice really, and your name was in Catherine McKenzie's diary. Georgina, Catherine's partner, thought you were probably the best person for me to contact."

Not wanting to give too much away and lay myself open, I began quite cautiously to explain the outline of my brief association with Catherine.

"I was helping Catherine with an investigation she was working on before her untimely death last week in Afghanistan."

"You're a reporter are you?"

"No, my involvement was quite involuntary."

Again without elaborating, I continued.

"Catherine asked me to accompany her on a trip to Germany. She was attempting to meet up with someone who was in possession of some papers he'd come across in Iraq. Apparently they contained information not only relative to the story she'd been working on, but also of interest to our security services."

John Williams looked me up and down. He needed to know more. He needed to verify in his own mind the authenticity of his guest. Was he genuine? Or was his visit this morning simply to tap into his reserves of expertise and if so, for whom?

"I think a drink may help, Mr Murray. Will you join me?"

Without waiting for my reply he walked over to the desk, grabbed one of the unopened bottles of wine, unscrewed the top and filled two glasses.

Pushing the books and papers covering the two chairs onto the floor, he handed me my drink. It was a bit early for me but not wanting to offend, I took the glass.

"Right, take a seat James. I need to know a little more before I can tell you whether I can be of any help or not. Firstly, how long have you known Catherine?"

"The first time we met was a couple of weeks ago, after I returned from a business trip in Paris."

I decided I wasn't going to get very far unless I came clean and told the full story. The bizarre events in Paris, my meeting with Catherine in Birmingham, the letter which had fallen out of the attaché case thrown at me from the car which had nearly run me down. I relayed all this information, but kept to my alias.

"So James, you've got yourself well and truly caught up in the murky waters not only of our secret service, but the media industry as well. I've never been able to decide which of the two are more lethal. The media I think." John took another swig and stared at his glass. "Yes, my money is on the media."

Getting up from his chair, he poured another glass of wine and handed me the bottle.

"No more for me, I've hardly started this one yet."

"Okay, what else can you tell me?"

"That's about everything. There is one thing that puzzles me though. You're a journalist. Is it normal for someone in your profession to work with MI6? I'd have thought, with the greatest respect, anyone in your profession would be the very last person MI6 would take into their confidence."

"More often than not it's the other way around. The media probably holds as many secrets as MI6. Our surveillance operatives, detection expertise, and methods are every bit as good as theirs – if not better on occasions. Our organisations are in bed with politicians, cabinet ministers, prime ministers, and police forces, right up to chief constables – not to mention the heads of the world's security organisations. We can, and often do, literally choose who'll be the next prime minister. Yes, the media organisations work with our security services on occasions. As a war correspondent, Catherine would no doubt have been asked for assistance from time to time, sharing information, that sort of thing. Robert Maxwell's body was found floating in the Atlantic. Not because he killed himself but because of his vast amount of knowledge. He was a superspy for Mossad, Israel's intelligence organisation. He asked them for £400 million to help get him out of the financial difficulties he found himself in, which they refused. Then fearing he would retaliate by exposing them, they assassinated him – using nerve gas, apparently. I recommend you read the book *The Assassination of Robert Maxwell: Israel's Superspy*. Our secret service and the media are very closely knit. They don't perhaps acknowledge that fact but trust me, they are. These days it's the Murdochs and News International, among others."

John poured himself another glass from the now half-empty bottle. Anxious to get as many of my questions answered as possible before my host became too intoxicated, I continued.

"Were you reporting in Iraq at the time Catherine was there?"

"No, I gave up gadding about all over the world a couple of months before 9/11. Twenty years reporting from Bosnia, Rwanda, and the West Bank, among other places, was enough. Missed out on all the fun since 9/11, or so I'm told. But my wife is much happier now. If I'm honest, so am I. Spend my time writing now – novels mostly. A mix of the truth and fantasy and, unlike in the real world, I can delete or change characters and events at the touch of a button. My wife enjoyed a successful career in the city so we don't have to worry about money.

"Catherine worked with me for just over six years. She was a bright girl, and a very capable journalist. Imaginative, hard-working – she'd pursue any story she was working on to the ends of the earth to get what she wanted. Her only fault, if you can call it that, was that she was a little naïve – or maybe she just gave that impression, I'm not sure."

John looked deep in thought, then poured himself another drink.

"I'll make some phone calls James, see what I can dig up. Leave this with me for a while."

"Thanks, I'd appreciate any advice you can give. By the way, do you know anything about a company called BAOR?"

My question seemed to catch his attention.

"British and American Oil Refineries? Why do you ask?"

"I'm not absolutely sure but I think I saw a letterhead or compliments slip with their logo at Sir David Gough's apartment when Catherine and I returned from Germany. It may be nothing but I can't seem to get it out of my head. In fact, I'm absolutely positive now that I saw the same logo on an envelope at Heidi's apartment – Snowstorm's girlfriend."

"That could be interesting, James. I'll make some enquiries, see what I can find."

I wrote down my mobile number then got a taxi to Paddington station.

Chapter 27

I arrived back in Birmingham at 2.15pm and drove to Solihull. I needed time to think. I parked in the multi-storey car park at Touchwood again and walked to the town square. I got a coffee from Costa and sat outside. The sun was warm and the usual lunchtime custom had subsided.

I sat at one of the tables and tried to make sense of things. Why did the police, or whoever they were, turn up to arrest me at Broadcasting House? Who'd telephoned them to inform them a James Murray was calling to discuss the investigation Catherine had been working on? Was it MI6? Had Sir David Gough got news someone was asking questions? From all that I was learning, especially this morning after my meeting with John Williams, it could be just about anyone. The situation was as sensitive as anything I could have ever imagined, not to mention complicated.

My mobile bleeped, it was a text from John Williams: Call me. I have some interesting news.

I walked over to Warwick Road and telephoned him from the call box there.

"I've managed to get some information which may be of interest, Michael. Firstly, three people at Broadcasting House who were working with Catherine have been arrested by Special Branch. I don't have any more details on that at the moment but I'll keep you posted. Now, the really interesting news is about BAOR. I'm informed by a very reliable source that Sir David Gough is closely associated with the company, and rumour has it he's been paid several million in consultancy fees so far and is planning to retire soon from MI6 and take up the post of European Operations Director."

I was right then about the logo I'd seen at Sir David's apartment. The information John had dug up for me was beginning to make sense. A pattern of sorts was beginning to emerge. One which was beginning to give a totally different angle on Operation Aries.

"John, thank you for that. And by the way, how did you discover my real name?"

"Michael, I've been in the business of uncovering secrets all my working life. It wasn't difficult. One piece of advice though: be very wary. Watch your back."

"I've no choice have I? I'll let you know how things develop, and thanks again."

I hung up and walked back to my table outside the Costa coffee house. The table was still unoccupied and my half-full cup still there. I sat down and opened up the diary Georgina had given me. As I sipped the lukewarm coffee, I looked again at the cryptic message Georgina had pointed out to me. The one Catherine believed held the answers, the final piece of the jigsaw.

The bad weather is now over.
Everyone loves Mozart.
857753770

Chapter 28

Looking again at the cryptic message Catherine had written, I wondered what the numbers represented. Was this another safe combination? It can't be a telephone number starting with 857, unless... Unless it had been written in reverse.

I took out my mobile and dialled the number in reverse. There was no tone. I had an idea. I called the operator and got the dialling code for Vienna. I dialled the code, then the number again. The phone was ringing. I immediately switched it off, removed the back cover, took out the SIM card and threw it into one of the waste bins as I walked over to the Car Phone store and purchased a new card. I walked back to the phone box I'd just used to call John Williams. I was still uneasy about using my mobile, even though I'd just purchased a new SIM card. Holding a handful of change I dialled the number. The phone rang and was answered almost immediately.

"Hello, 0777357758."

It was a woman's voice. I poured more coins into the box. I had absolutely no idea what I was going to say. I thought about hanging up and trying again later but, I started to speak.

"Hello, I have some papers Catherine McKenzie asked me to bring over to you. Can you tell me if this would be convenient some time tomorrow afternoon?"

"Catherine, you say?"

"Yes, some papers which she said you'd want to read through."

"Papers about what? And who are you?"

"Sorry, didn't I say? My name is James Murray. I work from time to time for Catherine in her work at the BBC. As I'm in Vienna tomorrow she asked if I would mind dropping these in to you."

"What are they?"

"I've really no idea except she did tell me they were important and thought you'd want to see them. She didn't want to risk posting them and as I'm in Vienna tomorrow she asked me to drop them over to you."

"You're in Vienna tomorrow, you say?"

"Yes, just passing through. Tomorrow afternoon."

"Ring me again tomorrow then."

How exactly I'd managed all that I wasn't sure, but it seemed to have worked. The problem was I had absolutely no idea who the woman was that I'd just spoken to, what her relationship with Catherine was – if any – and where in Vienna she was living. But I was going to find out. The only thing I'd discovered so far was that she spoke good English with a German accent. All I could do was get a flight to Vienna and call her again tomorrow.

Chapter 29

I drove back to Birchwood House and packed a case. Theresa was looking after everything in her usual and very capable way. Gordon was getting on well with the new assistant and Gary and his team were busy finishing off the bathrooms and kitchens in the barns. Carol was spending a couple of days with her sister in London who was about to give birth to her second child. And I, I thought, am about to make one big effort to get to the bottom of Operation Aries and then get back to what I should be doing: looking after my business, decorating and generally putting all my efforts into Birchwood House Farm and MCL Carriers.

Remembering what Catherine had told me about how anyone under surveillance is kept tabs on, I decided to book a flight to Paris and from there, a train to Vienna. If I was being watched then I was going to cover my back every way I could think of. I made a call to the transport director of Les Machines and told him I was in Paris tomorrow and would like to see him to go over the possibility of using space at the side of their factory at Nantes as a depot for some of our trucks. This was something we'd already talked about but thought it would give my visit to Paris an authentic reason to anyone who may just be tapping into my calls.

After checking out a few things at the office and signing some cheques, I told Theresa I'd see her later in the week, Friday at the latest. Then I'd get all the accounts sorted out and pay the contractors for the refurbishment work. The new alarms and security lights had all been fitted and I was more relaxed at leaving Birchwood House Farm unattended at night.

My flight took off from Birmingham at just turned 5pm and we landed at Charles de Gaulle airport at 7.25pm. In an effort to give my trip more cover, I even booked a room at the Hotel Campanile. Having checked in and spoken briefly to the receptionist, Claudine, I went to my room, showered, put on a change of clothes and ordered a taxi to take me to Gare de l'Est. A train was leaving for Vienna at 10.15pm, which should arrive at 9am the following morning. This, would perhaps give me time to plan my meeting with the mystery woman I'd spoken to yesterday afternoon. I grabbed a sandwich and a can of Coke from the station cafeteria and boarded the train. I was down to my last couple of cigarettes which I smoked during the journey by leaning out of the train window. It wasn't too embarrassing – there were three other passengers going through exactly the same routine. I reminded myself I'd need to buy a couple of packs when we reached Vienna.

I didn't sleep during the ten-hour journey but did manage to relax. The seats were considerably more comfortable than those I'd experienced on our trains back home.

We pulled into Vienna station at just turned 9.15am. I walked across the platform and into a cafeteria. I ordered scrambled egg on toast, a coffee, and as the cafeteria sold cigarettes, I got myself a couple of packs.

I finished the scrambled egg on toast, grabbed my coffee and walked out onto the platform. Sitting on one of the benches, I lit a cigarette, took another swig of coffee and began to think through the best way to approach things from here on in.

So far, I'd been extremely lucky. I'd spoken to a woman but had no idea what connection she had with Catherine McKenzie or Operation Aries, if any. I'd not the faintest idea of who she was. I'd mentioned Catherine whom I assumed she knew, and told her I had some papers I wanted to deliver to her today. She hadn't questioned me about anything. As it was obvious she knew Catherine, was she a friend of hers? A colleague, in the same sort of journalistic work? Or was she an agent working for the KGB, or possibly one of those rogue agents Catherine had described to me? I simply had no idea. Remembering the last encounter with members of the opposition on our visit to Hamburg, I was aware I needed to plan a meeting with some sort of escape route. The first thing was to telephone the mystery woman and find out where she lived. At the moment, I thought it could be half a mile or a hundred miles away.

I looked at my watch: 10.15am. Still not wishing to use my mobile I walked over to one of the public phone booths, put a handful of euros on the shelf next to the phone and dialled her number.

The phone was answered almost immediately.

"Hello, I called yesterday – James Murray. I'm in Vienna at the moment. If you'd like me to drop off these papers Catherine gave me, I can call over now if it's convenient."

"Mr Murray, I take it you are aware Catherine McKenzie was killed by a landmine in Afghanistan a couple of days ago."

"Yes, I know. I heard the news. Look, I don't know what these papers are she gave me before leaving for Afghanistan, but I got the impression they are quite important. Anyway, what do you want me to do? Shall I drop them over to you or just leave it?"

I was pushing my luck. I knew it, but I somehow thought if this woman had any connection with Catherine she'd be unable to resist taking delivery of something I hoped sounded important.

"My address is Medekstrasse 140. I have to go out later this morning so if you can bring them over to me straight away then I'll be here. If not just leave them in the porch."

I had no idea how far Medekstrasse was but I'd soon find out.

"Right, I'll be over shortly. Thank you."

I scooped the remaining euros off the shelf, dropping a couple on the floor of the booth in the process, which I didn't bother to scramble for. I walked out of the station and over to one of the taxis parked outside.

Leaning through the window of one of the cabs, I asked the driver to take me to Medekstrasse. Again the language barrier came into play. Same obstacle I'd had in Paris. But eventually understanding his reply, I climbed into the cab. A thirty-minute drive later we arrived at Medekstrasse. I paid the driver and walked past number 140, a large detached property in what was obviously a very upmarket area. I looked around. Then, as unobtrusively as possible, walked down to the end of the road, turned right and began to walk back along the same route my taxi had taken. About a three-mile walk later I entered the high street of the town we'd passed through earlier. I went into a cafeteria, ordered a cup of coffee and asked if I could use their phone. The owner here spoke perfect English – my hand signals and miming techniques were not required. I dialled the number of the mystery woman and put part one of my plan into action. Part one was to meet with this woman in a public place. Somewhere I would not be cornered, in case of an unfriendly reception. Again, my experiences in Germany were at the forefront of my mind. I was, albeit in perhaps a rather amateurish way, attempting to cover my back. I knew I had to gamble, go with my instincts and just hope for the best.

Chapter 30

I still had absolutely no idea who the woman was I was about to meet up with, or where she came from, or what connection she may have had to Operation Aries, if any. The only thing I knew was that Catherine had written down this woman's telephone number, together with a cryptic message regarding the weather, which may or may not have been a reference to Snowstorm.

I made the call and used the excuse that my car had broken down. I said that while waiting for the arrival of a mechanic I was at the Café Florianihof, just a couple of miles away. The mystery woman seemed somewhat annoyed but said she'd drive over and meet me there in ten to fifteen minutes.

I'd taken a table close to the rear exit doors, just in case a quick exit was called for. There were around a dozen people in the café who I assumed were mostly local business people using the place for their coffee break – apart from one of the tables near the front, occupied by a young woman battling to keep her three children under control. Playing in the background was one of the symphonies composed by the city's most famous of sons, Mozart. There were also several large posters dotted around advertising the music festival being held at the Klosterneuburg Concert Hall.

After almost half an hour a tall, slim, twenty-something, very attractive woman walked into the café. She seemed to identify me almost immediately. She walked towards my table and sat down opposite me. She was both younger and prettier than I had imagined, and seemed a lot more relaxed than the rather short conversations had indicated.

"Thank you for coming to see me. Can I get you a drink?"

"No thank you, Mr Murray. You said you have some papers for me?"

I could think of no other way to proceed than to be totally upfront and explain everything.

"I have a confession to make. In fact, more than one confession. My name is Michael McLoughlan, not James Murray. I helped Catherine McKenzie a couple of weeks ago in her efforts to locate someone in Germany, someone who'd been working for the same organisation she was connected to in England. The person she was attempting to make contact with held information, or at least knew the whereabouts of information which Catherine was attempting to secure in her work as an investigative journalist. As you are aware, Catherine was killed the other day in Afghanistan when compiling a news report for the BBC and I'm trying to put together the loose ends of the work she was involved with before her untimely death."

One of the waitresses approached our table and I ordered another coffee. I was becoming somewhat unnerved by the almost glacial look in the eyes of the woman sitting opposite me.

"Please continue, Mr McLoughlan."

I was not only working totally in the dark but wondered if I'd already said too much. I still had no idea who this woman was. I began to feel awkward and somewhat deflated. I glanced around the cafeteria. Any one of the people there could be a surveillance operative – or was I just being paranoid?

Before I'd decided how to continue the mystery woman spoke.

"Let me see if I can help you. You say you accompanied Catherine to Germany last month when she called at my apartment to speak with me?"

"You're Heidi? You met Catherine at the Alder Coffee House?"

"Yes, Mr McLoughlan. My name is Heidi Gantevoort and I spoke briefly with Catherine McKenzie – not in her role as a journalist but as you are no doubt well aware, in her role as an agent for your secret service organisation, MI6. That's who you're working for is it not?"

"No Heidi, I have absolutely nothing at all to do with them. I'm simply a friend of Catherine's and I'm attempting to put together a few loose ends she never had the time to finish. I'm aware all of this probably sounds very suspicious but it's the truth."

Heidi gave me a long hard stare.

"Actually it was obvious to me you weren't connected with MI6, Mr McLoughlan. But I'm still not convinced of either who you are or what you want from me. If you're looking for Brian – or 'Snowstorm' as that bunch of murderers in London referred to him – then you're too late. He's dead. They murdered him before we had time to leave Germany. So come on, tell me what exactly is it you want from me?"

Heidi was not only angry but appeared to be on the edge of breaking down. The music seemed to be getting louder, as were the children at the front of the café.

"Look Heidi, can we talk outside somewhere? Will you give me a few minutes to explain things?"

Without answering, Heidi obviously agreeing with my suggestion, got up from the table. I followed her outside.

"I like Mozart, Michael, but not all day, every fucking day."

I smiled.

"Come on, let's walk along while I try to explain things."

"Before you start, Michael, tell me, if you're not associated with your security services, which I actually have no problem in believing, how did you become involved with Catherine McKenzie?"

"I was in Paris a month ago on business. Walking back to the hotel I was almost knocked down by a stolen car. As the car passed me an attaché case was thrown from the car which I later discovered contained papers giving the location of some photographs taken in Iraq just before the invasion. That was when Catherine contacted me. After explaining a few things to me she asked if she could accompany me on one of the deliveries I was making in Hamburg. She explained that she needed to speak with one of their agents, Snowstorm, who was apparently working for MI6 in Iraq prior to the invasion. I dropped Catherine off then went on to make my delivery. When I returned she said she'd managed to meet you, but had still not made contact with their agent. After that we were sidetracked somewhat by a rather unpleasant couple of characters who tried very hard to make our visit to Germany the very last. Eventually we got back to England and that was the last time I saw Catherine. The problem I have now Heidi, is as Catherine pointed out to me at our very first meeting, my life and the life of anyone else who is even suspected of having any connection with all this business – Operation Aries, as it's called – are in danger of being eliminated. So I must confess my visit here does have a selfish interest. I'm not just trying to tie up all the loose ends for nothing, I'm trying to figure out a way of putting an end to the threat which I believe is hanging over me. Not only me, but you, and anyone else who has knowledge of the story."

We continued walking down the high street, passing all the shops and cafeterias and coming eventually to an area of grassland overlooking the river. We stood for a moment in silence, watching some children throwing bread for the ducks. Just like our local park back home, I thought. Heidi looked deep in thought, then shrugging her shoulders, turned to me.

"I may as well tell you everything. The problem is, I doubt it will help much. The best I can hope for is that it makes life a little more unpleasant for all those bastards involved in this maze of deceit with their self-centred interests. I met Brian just over six years ago, when I was working in England as a translator for a company in

Coventry. After we got to know each other he eventually told me he worked with MI6 but he didn't elaborate on what his work involved and I never asked him. Before the invasion of Iraq, the time when all the weapons inspectors were going backwards and forwards and both Bush and Blair were busy making the case for invading the country, Brian was sent to Iraq to dig out any information that could possibly help in strengthening the case for war. There were several agents working there, both from MI6 and other countries. His code name, as you know, was Snowstorm. After the bombing raids and before Saddam was found hiding in a hole somewhere, Brian gained access to one of Saddam's palaces which had been partly destroyed by the bombing. In one of the rooms, he and two of his colleagues discovered several filing cabinets full of papers and correspondence between Saddam's regime, Colonel Gaddafi and both the British and American governments. These letters confirmed the West's intention to help keep the dictators of these countries in place in exchange for deals on oil supplies. Brian also found photographs filed along with all the other papers. The photographs showed some of the weapons the West had supplied to these regimes as part of the ongoing deal they'd agreed upon to keep them in power. These dictators were aware their regimes were under threat from the growing discontent of their people. They knew they needed help if they were to stand any chance of remaining in control. The problem, however, was Saddam. He was the loose cannon. After the invasion of Kuwait it became obvious the British and American governments were dealing with someone who was totally unreliable – a dictator who they would never be able to do a deal with, unlike Gaddafi or any of the others they were in contact with. These letters and photographs Brian brought back with him from Iraq confirmed the lengths the West had been prepared to go to in keeping these tyrants in power to secure the oil deals they were after. You know, Michael, everything creates a shadow. The shadows created by the people Brian worked for, the people who so sanctimoniously dictate to us what's right or what's acceptable, create the very darkest of shadows. And they need to. The shadows they create have to hide the very worst of human nature."

Heidi looked almost in tears. I looked into her eyes and saw how the death of her boyfriend Brian and all that was going on had taken away an enormous part of this very lovely young woman.

"What about the £1 million Heidi? The money Brian was paid by MI6 for the return of the original photographs and all the correspondence he brought back with him?"

"There was no million pound payment nor any request made for one. Brian wasn't trying to blackmail anyone. That was all part of a story being created by MI6 to discredit anything he might have revealed about the discoveries made in Iraq. He was aware arrangements had already been made to have negatives created to make the photographs look as though they'd been faked. That, together with the so-called blackmail attempt, had been created to undermine anything he may have revealed. All he was attempting to do was to get us somewhere safe. He was holding on to the photographs and papers as a bargaining tool, as some sort of security. He told me that Sir David Gough, the head of your secret service, had arranged for us to move to Canada. We had the promise of a house and a lucrative position for Brian at a company Sir David was a director of, but Brian was worried. He told me he couldn't trust anything he'd been told. Two of his former colleagues in Iraq who'd also seen the documents had been killed. He knew there was no one he could trust, and he was right.

Brian knew Catherine had been recruited by MI6. He knew she'd been investigating the discovery of the photographs and the letters discovered in Iraq. He was also aware she was simply being used by MI6 because her knowledge of the situation was useful to them, but he knew as soon as they'd got what they wanted she'd probably be eliminated. Anyway, Brian asked me to tell her he was visiting his sister and then going to see a few friends before we flew out to Canada."

"So the letter in the attaché case? Was that just part of the attempt by MI6 to make it look like Brian was blackmailing them?"

"No, when Brian was attempting to do a deal with Sir David Gough he was asked to give the location of all the photographs and papers. Brian left a letter giving the location, to be collected from a second-hand shop in Paris. However, he'd only sent copies to the location he detailed. He didn't trust the people he was negotiating with, he was just buying time."

I looked at the ducks chasing the pieces of bread thrown to them by the children standing at the side of the lake and thought how lucky they were. The only thing they had to worry about was eating and looking after their young. It seemed they'd got it right. It was the rest of us who seemed hell-bent on making life so bloody complicated.

"You're young Heidi, and beautiful. You'll build a new life for yourself. You need to look beyond all this, begin to make some plans for your future."

"What future, Michael? Even when I can begin to get over all that's happened, what have I got? A life looking over my shoulder? A life not knowing if today is the day one of the thugs hired by your intelligence service, or any intelligence service, will make their hit and collect the £1,000 or whatever the going rate is these days for dealing with what they call an unacceptable risk."

All the time Heidi had been explaining things to me, I'd been thinking. Even if my knowledge of our security services was unknown territory for me there was one thing I was absolutely certain of: the people involved would only back off when they knew they were beaten – when they knew there was no further gain for them. Just like the real world. The problem was, how would we beat this assortment of characters we'd come up against? I had an idea I'd been mulling over on the journey from Paris. I thought – I certainly hoped – it might just be the answer.

"Heidi, there is possibly a way out of this. Firstly, tell me, do you have the photographs and the letters Brian brought back with him?"

Heidi hesitated for a moment.

"A few days ago, Michael, there wasn't a person living I'd give this information to. But now, now I'm almost past caring. Yes, I have the papers – all of them, and the photographs. If you want them, you're welcome to them. I'll get them for you."

Chapter 31

We walked back to the high street, to the car Heidi had parked a couple of hundred yards from the Café Florianihof, and began the drive back to Medekstrasse.

"Who are you staying with Heidi?"

"My ex-boyfriend and his partner. We've remained good friends and they've both been very supportive. And before you say anything, I'm as safe there as anywhere else. Absolutely no one knows where I am. I can assure you of that."

"Alright Heidi, but be careful. It might be an idea if you drop me off before we get there and I'll walk round."

"No, it's okay. I know a little of how surveillance operations work. We're okay, for a while anyway."

I accepted Heidi's assurances.

"And your plan is what, Michael, when you have all the papers?"

"Make copies and post them to my solicitors in England and one other contact of mine. They'll have instructions to release them to every major newspaper and media outlet in the event of either you, Georgina or myself not surviving the next fifty years or so. I'll hand over the originals together with an explanation of my insurance plan to Sir David Gough at MI6, with a promise not to reveal anything, including his interest in British and American Oil Refineries. That's my plan Heidi."

"Will that wash? Do you really think that'll work?"

"I don't see why not. After all, the idea of blackmail comes from MI6. I'm a businessman. Have been since I left school. Everything we've looked at and discovered so far has been complicated to say the least. My bet is that the offer of a very simple deal will be accepted. To be honest Heidi, I can't think of an alternative plan. It's the only thing we've got to bargain with. For obvious reasons the security services of both this country and the United States want these papers and photographs under lock and key. Well, that's fine. They can have them, all of them, but with the knowledge that should any one of us end up dead somewhere, then their secret will be revealed to the world. I've always tried to put myself in the place of the person I'm negotiating with. Now if I was Sir David Gough, or indeed anyone else involved in this business, then I think I'd accept an offer like that. After all, the way I see it, I'd have no alternative would I?"

"I hope you're right, Michael."

"That makes two of us."

We pulled up outside 140 Medekstrasse. I walked through into the hallway with Heidi and waited while she went to collect the papers. Returning to the hallway, she handed me an A4 envelope.

"Everything is in there, the whole bloody lot."

"Heidi, the sooner I'm away from here the better for all of us. I'll telephone you in the next couple of days, I promise." I turned and looked at this battered and deflated young woman. "You just hang on a few days Heidi. I'll call you, that's a promise."

Heidi didn't reply immediately. She just looked at me, then with the slightest of smiles said "Good luck."

I walked back down Medekstrasse, took out my mobile and the card I'd picked up from the taxi I'd used earlier and ordered a cab to take me back to Vienna station. I needed to make photocopies of the papers and photographs Heidi had given me. I was aware that the sooner copies of these documents were on their way to my contacts the better. Fortunately my taxi driver spoke perfect English. He drove me to one of the large stores he knew had copiers for customer use. I ran the papers and photographs through the machine. I paid for the photocopies and purchased some A4 envelopes and a pack of writing paper containing six smaller envelopes. I put the originals back in the envelope Heidi had given me, sat down at one of the desks beside the copier and wrote the same letter to the contacts. Contacts with whom I was about to entrust a collection of the most explosive secrets since the height of the Cold War. There was one for the principal of Gainsborough & Partners, my solicitors in Solihull who'd handled all my conveyancing projects over the past few years and one to John Hammond, principal partner of Hammond Wainwright and Peters, the solicitors who'd handled my divorce some eight years previously. I knew both of these people well. I'd kept in touch with them both in a business and personal way over the years. I knew the confidentiality of the papers and my letter would be assured. I was desperately trying to get down on paper, as quickly as possible, instructions for the safe keeping of the information I was about to mail. The photocopiers were situated beside the main entrance to the store and I was standing at the desk next to these while trying to write my instruction letters. People were passing by me, coming in and out of the store. A couple of young children bumped into me, causing a scribbled line to appear on one of the letters, but I managed to finish the task. I put the copies and my instruction letters into the envelopes and walked over to the post office opposite to post both letters. I placed a short note I'd also written in one of the smaller envelopes. I put this in my inside jacket pocket.

I went back to my taxi and nodded at the driver who was busy reading one of the local papers. We continued the drive to Vienna station.

It was 5.15pm when we arrived. My train to Paris was not due to leave until 6pm. I settled my fare with the driver together with a twenty euro tip for his patience and help in finding me the stationery store. I walked up the long concrete stairway of the station to a low-ceilinged platform housing several shops and two cafeterias. I showed the return ticket I'd purchased in Paris the day before to the ticket inspector standing at the iron-gated entrance. There were several dozen people, all waiting for the arrival of the night train to Paris. I guessed they were mainly holidaymakers and people who'd been attending one of the many concerts and tours celebrating the city's most famous son, Wolfgang Amadeus Mozart. I really didn't know why the Viennese people made out Mozart was one of theirs. He didn't move to Vienna until 1781 at the age of thirty-five and died a few years later. But it was good for business so why not, I thought. I'd often heard theories that Shakespeare wasn't the author of all the works accredited to him but it made no difference really. Stratford-upon-Avon thrives upon it being his birthplace and generates millions every year from tourism, plus of course, the Shakespeare Memorial Theatre, one of the most famous theatres in the world. I got myself a coffee and sat down on one of the benches on the platform. I sipped the coffee and smoked a cigarette. I was busy going over the plan I'd put into action. A plan I hoped would take away the threat of being bumped off one day by one of the assassins hired so easily by any one of the many security organisations interested in the information obtained by Heidi's boyfriend. I had to not only take the danger from me, but from Georgina and Heidi as well. My mind was working overtime on all that had happened – not only over the past couple of days but ever since I'd picked up that bloody attaché case in Paris. My plan should work, I reasoned. In any case, I could think of no other way to secure our safety.

Our train pulled up alongside the platform and seemed to sigh as it came to a halt. I thought I'd try to get a carriage close to the dining car. I was both tired and hungry. While deciding on the carriage to use, I was oblivious to two people who'd been observing me since I walked onto the platform. There was a tall guy wearing a pair of heavy dark-rimmed glasses. Then a little further along the platform was a young, rather scruffily dressed backpacker wearing jeans, trainers, and an anorak and carrying a large haversack over his shoulders.

Chapter 32

Our train pulled out of the station just as I was settling into one of the carriages. There were fewer passengers than yesterday and I had the carriage to myself. The train seemed to hum along the tracks as if, like me, it was preparing itself for the ten-hour journey ahead. I settled back into the seat and decided when I reached Paris I'd try to get a few hours' sleep at my room at the Hotel Campanile. I was determined to get something for the bill I'd be greeted with tomorrow.

A couple of hours into the journey I made my way to the dining car and was shown to a table by one of the smartly dressed waiters. I ordered the grilled salmon with new potatoes and salad and a double whisky and soda. The meal was good and I concluded with a further double whisky and soda. I paid for the meal on my Visa card and walked back to my compartment. I closed and locked the door, pulled down the blinds, opened the window slightly and lit a cigarette. After the cigarette I closed the window, sat back in the seat and closed my eyes. I was tired, I'd eaten, I'd had a cigarette, so maybe I'd get some sleep.

I was woken by a knock on the carriage door. I looked at my watch: 2.30am – almost halfway through the journey. A second knock came, this time a little louder.

"We have a problem with the train. We'll need to change over at Strasbourg. I need to check your ticket for the changeover."

I unlocked the carriage door and began to slide it back when suddenly it swept back. A tall, thick-set character pushed into the carriage holding what looked like some relic of a pistol from the Second World War. It was too late for me to counteract the guy's intentions. I stood looking at him as he closed the door behind him. How could I have been so stupid?

"Sit down, Mr McLoughlan. I'm here for one thing and one thing only: the envelope."

I was about to start the process of stalling the guy, asking the obvious questions: What envelope? Who are you? What do you want? You've obviously got the wrong person...

Instinct told me that was not the way to proceed. Not with this guy. I'd have to look for a better opportunity.

"It's in my coat pocket," I said, pointing to the luggage rack above my head.

"Get it for me, Mr McLoughlan."

As I stood up to get the coat I was still trying to work out if there was any way of disarming the guy. Should I try making a grab for the gun as I reached for my coat? No, he was standing at the back of the carriage by the door, holding the pistol directly at me. There was no doubt in my mind that the slightest movement from me to make a move towards him would bring an abrupt end to all my plans for a long and successful life. He was in control and would have no hesitation in pulling the trigger of the rather antique, but nevertheless very deadly-looking weapon he was continuing to point directly at me. He had the upper hand, for the moment anyway. I reached for my coat, took out the A4 envelope from the inside pocket and handed it him.

"Whoever has sent you to collect this may like to know copies are held at two very safe locations. Should anything happen to me or any of the people involved in all this crap then those copies will be forwarded to every newspaper and media organisation around the world."

"I'm just paid to collect the envelope, Mr McLoughlan. What happens after that, I really couldn't care less."

It was obvious there was no way of negotiating with the guy. It was also obvious, even to an amateur like me, that he was not employed by MI6. He was freelancing. He was, as he said, simply paid to get the envelope.

I hoped his instructions didn't include any final plans for me. My mind was working on overtime. I'd noticed he hadn't locked the carriage door. Was there a way I could distract him and get that pistol off him without being blasted halfway back to Vienna?

These thoughts were suddenly interrupted as the carriage door swung open. A scruffy individual in jeans, trainers, and a very unclean looking anorak stood in the doorway.

"Sorry mate, wrong carriage."

Suddenly, this scruffy individual, dropped to his knees pointing what I recognised as a 13mm Gyrojet pistol directly at the large stocky fellow opposite me who'd been demanding the envelope.

The large stocky fellow opposite froze. Staring at the pistol pointing directly at his head. It was obvious he had no intention of being a hero.

"Michael, get the gun."

The young, scruffy backpacker was Catherine McKenzie. I took the pistol from my intruder.

"Cover him, Michael."

Catherine closed the carriage door and locked it.

"Catherine! Where the hell did you come from?"

She smiled, then turned to speak to the intruder standing opposite me.

"We have about twenty minutes before reaching Strasbourg where we are scheduled to make a stop. You will get off and make contact with your employers, whoever they may be. You'll tell them there was no Michael McLoughlan on this train and no documents, do you understand?"

"And what makes you think I'll do that?"

"I think you will. It'll sound a lot better than telling them we disarmed you, took your wallet, your mobile, all your identity papers, all your money, your coat and jacket, and left you in your shirt sleeves on the platform of Strasbourg Station, which is what is about to happen. All that will not look good on your CV will it? Not to mention the action whoever employed you might decide to take. But the choice is yours – now take off your coat and jacket and empty your pockets."

The guy was seething, but he had the sense to know he had no choice. Taking off his coat and jacket he emptied his pockets onto the seat behind him.

"Your wristwatch as well if you don't mind. Michael, check him over."

I checked the guy over. Standing there in his shirt sleeves, he knew he was well and truly beaten. It would take him some time to make his way back to wherever he came from and I doubted he'd admit to being made a fool of – I reckoned he'd not say anything except that there was no Michael McLoughlan, nor were there any papers to be found. I felt our train begin to slow down as we crept into Strasbourg station. Catherine took off her anorak and placed it over the Gyrojet pistol she was holding.

"This is your station."

Following a safe distance behind, Catherine waited as the guy disembarked from the train. After a few minutes our train pulled out of Strasbourg station to continue the remaining six hours of our journey to Paris.

Chapter 33

Catherine returned to the carriage and went through the contents left on the seat by the intruder. Then bundling them all together, she opened the carriage window and threw them out.

I looked at Catherine. As relieved as I was at being rescued from what was probably going to be the end game for me, I had questions I wanted answers to.

"Okay, are you going to tell me what the hell is going on? I'm very grateful for your sudden intrusion here but correct me if I'm wrong, you're supposed to be dead aren't you? Blown up somewhere in Afghanistan. So come on, how about explaining things?"

Catherine smiled at me.

"So you're glad to see me then, Michael?"

"Of course I am. And thank you for probably saving my life a few moments ago. However, I'd rather be watching you making one of your reports on television than worrying about you running around all over the place dodging bombs and bullets everywhere. So come on, update me. Then I'll tell you what I've arranged to hopefully put an end to this nightmare."

"Well, you won't have to keep worrying about me dodging bombs and bullets, as you put it, for much longer. You'll be pleased to know I've decided to give up my work as a war correspondent, including any further assignments with MI6. I'm going for something a little more homely." Catherine smiled. "I've been offered the job of presenting two new programmes being launched this autumn on Channel Four. I've decided to take up their offer. I'm going for a more quiet life, including a cottage in St Ives as soon as I've managed to achieve a sale on our house in Worcester. Then I can make sure Georgina has the opportunity of making a full recovery. I'll still be working all hours god sends but at least Georgina will know I won't be dodging bombs and bullets on my way home from the office every night."

Catherine sat back and stretched herself. Pushing back into the soft padding of the first class seating in our carriage she ran her fingers through her hair. She looked directly at me with her captivating blue eyes.

"However, there are things to finish and these are not going to be easy. I'm not clear yet on the best way forward."

It seemed to me as if this was the first time she'd seriously thought things through and had the opportunity to examine her life – examine all that she'd been through and all that was going on around her, not least of all Georgina's battle with cancer.

"Things get so fucking complicated, Michael. It just gets more and more difficult to know what is in fact true and what isn't. Anyway, enough about all that. I've made my decision to get away from all this once and for all. You made contact with Heidi then?"

"Yes, I met Georgina in Solihull. She showed me the notes you'd made in your diary and I telephoned Heidi and arranged to meet her. I had to bluff my way through everything. I didn't even know it was Heidi I was calling until earlier today. Anyway, she eventually gave me all the letters and photographs her boyfriend Brian, Snowstorm, had been holding onto."

"Did she explain to you that he wasn't attempting to blackmail MI6? When he discovered the photographs and the correspondence between the British and American governments, not to mention the correspondence between the Libyan government and everyone else, he quickly realised what he'd uncovered was so sensitive his life could be in danger. Then when two of his colleagues working with him in Iraq went missing, it confirmed his worst fears. Snowstorm tried to lie low for a while and hang onto the papers as some sort of security until he'd managed to find somewhere he'd be safe. He and Heidi moved to Germany, where we almost caught up with him. It was MI6 who made up the story of blackmail. They were desperately trying to undermine any possible story he might hand over to the press, or any other interested party come to that. They were apparently ready to make the photographs look suspect by having negatives made from the copies Brian had sent them. Then they made it look as though Brian had been demanding two million pounds plus a guarantee of safety in exchange for the originals and all the papers. My fears that anyone with knowledge of the photographs and letters found in Iraq were being killed off was confirmed during my visit to Afghanistan. When I was over there, as you can imagine, there were more security people surrounding the Prime Minister's visit than people actually involved in the visit itself. A jeep taking three of my team back to the helicopter hit a landmine. It was assumed I was in the vehicle. As it happened, fortunately for me, I'd decided to take a different route. Shortly after the accident one of my colleagues told me he'd overheard one of the security officers talking on his mobile, confirming there was no need now to worry about the instructions regarding me: the work had been taken care of by the Taliban. This revelation didn't exactly surprise me. I'd suspected for a while I was in a precarious situation. I'd been given a sealed operation to investigate. There was only a handful of people at MI6 who had full knowledge of what was going on. Rather conveniently, they were just using the knowledge of all I'd discovered in my investigations as war correspondent when working for the BBC in Afghanistan. Then, when you picked up that attaché case in Paris, they decided to encourage me to enlist your help as well. Anyway, I eventually managed to get out of

Afghanistan and then discovered there were in fact two operations in progress to recover the photographs and letters Snowstorm was holding onto – one by MI6 and another instigated by Whitehall. The two investigations overlapped. They tripped over each other which didn't exactly help things. Fortunately the operators being used in the government's investigation proved very amateurish. When you sent the letter you found in the attaché case to the address I gave you in London, it was intercepted. Intercepted on instructions from people in Whitehall who I've now found out have been using the services of a former CIA agent who runs a security company in London. He regularly employs the services of some of his old underworld contacts."

"Is it normal to have more than one investigation running like this, Catherine? Surely it's the job of MI6 to carry out this sort of investigation."

"Not with every investigation, and this one is not only big, but has uncovered a conflict of interests between MI6 and Downing Street. Over the years the government has been busy working at ways to safeguard our oil supplies and keep the dictators they deal with in place and…"

I interrupted.

"Sir David Gough has been busy keeping his interests with BAOR securely in place."

Catherine looked at me.

"You've found that out then?"

"I have, and my plan is to make it clear to Sir David Gough that if anything should happen to you, Georgina, Heidi or myself during the next fifty years or so then the copies I've made of all the photographs and letters your agent Snowstorm found in Iraq will be forwarded to every newspaper and media organisation around the world. They could issue as many D notices as they like but they wouldn't be able to prevent the story from breaking. I may be new to all this espionage business but as I see it, at the end of the day, deals can always be made. No different from the business world I've been involved with for the past fifteen years or so. At the end of the day everybody looks after their own interests. Deals are made to keep everyone happy."

"Michael, you do realise you'll probably get yourself arrested and charged with a multitude of offences under the official secrets act?"

"I don't think so. The MPs' expenses scandal was embarrassing enough. I doubt the government or our secret service would want to have to deal with the mountain of problems and backlash a story like this would create. Don't you think?

Anyway it's too late – copies of everything Snowstorm found in Iraq, including details of Sir David Gough's interest in British and American Oil Refineries, will be with contacts of mine with instructions to release the whole lot should anything happen to any of us."

Catherine looked thoughtful, staring out of the carriage window.

"It's possible it could work, but it's taking one hell of a risk."

"What alternative do we have? It's obvious everyone connected to this Aries operation, including me, is going to be systematically bumped off. As you are well aware, they'll get us sooner or later. So as I see it, we've absolutely nothing to lose."

Chapter 34

Our train pulled into Gare de l'Est at 8.15am, just over ten hours after leaving Vienna. We decided to return to the Hotel Campanile and keep our heads down for a while at the room I'd reserved there. Catherine could make arrangements for me to meet up with Sir David Gough in London, hopefully sometime later this evening. There was a flight from Charles de Gaulle airport at 6.15pm which was due to arrive at Heathrow at 8.20pm.

We took a taxi from the station and went straight to the hotel. After taking a shower I put on the change of clothes I'd brought with me. Catherine put on a towelling dressing gown (compliments of the Hotel Campanile) and unfolded a couple of dresses and a jacket she took from her rucksack. I poured us both a drink from the miniature bottles of whisky in the refrigerator. Adding ice and soda, I handed one to Catherine. I took the other and sat over by the window overlooking Rue du Faubourg Saint-Honoré.

I lit a cigarette and opened the window slightly to avoid setting off the hotel's smoke alarm system. Catherine pulled up a chair and joined me. We drank the whisky and soda and blew the cigarette smoke towards the open window. It was another warm sunny day. We looked out over Rue du Faubourg Saint-Honoré and listened to the traffic and the sound of car horns followed by the occasional screech of tyres as drivers pushed the limits of their driving abilities, or lack of them.

"If you'll make contact with Sir David today, Catherine, try and arrange a meeting for me this evening. The sooner we get our plan underway the better. I could go over to his apartment at River Lodge after we land at Heathrow."

"It'll be better to keep our location secret for a while longer, Michael. I'll make the call from the airport just before we board our flight."

"That lot at MI6 know by now you weren't killed by any landmine in Afghanistan, but do they have any idea where you are or what's happening?"

"They'll know by now how I got out of Afghanistan, but I doubt they'll have any idea either where I am or what identity I've been using. That's one thing I'm good at. I learnt a lot of the secrets from my old boss when working for a couple of the nationals. John Williams, he'd been working as a war correspondent for over twenty years. What he taught me during my time working with him has proved invaluable. In fact, if I hadn't had the benefit of all that experience I wouldn't be here now."

"I met John Williams, at his home in London. I got his number from the diary Georgina gave me. He was more than helpful, in fact he was the one who confirmed to me the connection between Sir David Gough and BAOR."

"That doesn't surprise me. He holds more information in that brain of his than anyone I've ever met – and anything he's not sure of he knows exactly who to ask. Anyway, how is the old rascal?"

"He seemed fine to me. Certainly likes his drink."

Catherine smiled.

"He always did. I must look him up when we get back home.

Now, when we book the flight it'll be safer for us to travel separately. I'll make the call to arrange your meeting with Sir David when we reach Charles de Gaulle airport. I'll give you the details and then from there it's best we travel separately."

I looked at my watch. It was 10.30am. I decided to try to get a couple of hours' sleep before our journey back to London, if at all possible. I telephoned Charles de Gaulle airport and booked our tickets: one for me and one in the name of Gillian Cooper, Catherine's alias. I then telephoned for a taxi to collect us at 4pm and take us to the airport.

"Catherine, would you do a couple of things for me? Firstly, would you let me have your bank details?"

"Bank details, Michael? What on earth for?"

"Don't ask questions. Just write them down on the pad over there. The other thing is about the guy who took over my room here a couple of weeks ago at the start of this escapade, Phillip Mason. I saw an article in one of the papers back home reporting his so-called heart attack. He was married with two children. I'd like to find out their address. Would you find that for me?"

"I can do that, but what for? What are you planning?"

"I'll tell you one day, if it all comes together. Now let's set the alarm for 3pm because I'd like to try to get a couple of hours' sleep before we set off."

"Good idea, Michael. I'll join you."

"This is the third time, Catherine, we've gone to bed together and kept our hands to ourselves."

Catherine smiled.

"Must be a record for you then?"

"I don't know about a record. More like a fucking miracle."

Catherine laughed. We were both asleep within minutes.

Chapter 35

The alarm woke me at 3.15pm. Catherine was already out of bed and dressed in her new attire: skirt, blouse and jacket. She was looking very sophisticated, totally the opposite from the scruffy backpacker outfit she'd been wearing earlier.

I scrambled out of bed, went to the bathroom, threw some water over my face, combed my hair, returned to the bedroom put on my jeans, shirt and shoes and joined Catherine by the window.

"Coffee, Michael?"

"Good idea. Do you know if they serve food on the plane or not?"

"They probably do but I doubt it's much good though."

"How about we get something to eat here before our taxi arrives?"

"Yes, okay then. I can't remember the last time I had anything to eat. All very good for the figure but it's getting past a joke now."

I went down to the reception, ordered some sandwiches, and settled my account. It was Claudine's day off, and there was no chance of any discount from the hotel manager who attended to the account and my request for sandwiches. After the usual niceties he wished me a safe journey and said he hoped I'd come back to the Hotel Campanile soon.

I went back to my room. We finished our sandwiches, had

one more coffee and cigarette each, then went down to reception, through the main entrance and out onto Rue du Faubourg and into the waiting taxi. We arrived at Charles de Gaulle airport and checked in for our flight back to Heathrow.

Some twenty minutes before boarding our plane Catherine disappeared to one of the public call boxes to arrange the meeting with Sir David Gough. A few minutes later she returned and told me the meeting had been agreed for 10pm, but not at Sir David's apartment. I was to meet him and Peter Astor at Thames Path, by Westminster Bridge. Catherine handed me the envelope containing the correspondence and photographs I'd collected from Heidi. She hesitated for a second then smiled.

"Thanks for all your help, and for being the perfect gentleman."

"That's alright. Let's just get our insurance plan underway. And as far as being the perfect gentleman, Catherine you did tell me on more than one occasion I was just not your type."

Catherine smiled, leant forward and kissed me.

"I might have been persuaded to change my mind, you never know."

I smiled back.

"Now you tell me."

We boarded the plane separately and sat through the journey as if complete strangers. We landed on time at Heathrow and after a brief and uneventful stroll through customs I walked into the enormous reception area. The PA system was busy giving details of arrivals and departures to the hundreds of passengers and visitors all looking anxious to escape the rain, which as always, I thought, was falling quite heavily. I walked out from the reception area and into one of the dozens of taxis waiting for their next fare.

"Thames Path, Westminster Bridge."

The driver nodded and we were on our way. By the time we'd arrived the rain had stopped. My driver commented it was just a brief shower and we'd actually been promised the possibility of a decent summer. I replied that I hoped so. We all certainly deserved one. Maybe this year, I thought, we may. I somehow felt optimistic about everything. I don't know where this feeling came from. I was about to attempt to strike a deal with the head of our secret service about probably one of the most sensitive incidents since the Cold War. However, the more I kept going over everything I'd discovered about Operation Aries, our government and MI6's involvement, the more confident I was that the deal I was about to put to Sir David Gough would be accepted. I really couldn't see what alternative he had. Whether that was wishful thinking or not, I wasn't sure. There was one thing I was sure about – I would very soon find out.

My taxi pulled up at Thames Path, just by the bridge. I paid the driver and walked over to one of the postboxes. I took out the envelope containing the note I'd written at the stationery shop in Vienna. I looked around then posted it in the box.

I walked the few hundred yards back to Thames Path and stood by the railings overlooking the Thames. It reflected the Palace of Westminster, all illuminated by the dozens of spotlights as if advertising to the whole world the power the place represented. The good, the bad and the ugly, I thought. But this place was the very centre of our democracy and for all its faults, I believed it had achieved the finest democracy in the world. However, like all great achievements the reality behind their creation was not always something to illuminate. That was the reality of things. I was hoping that very same reality would secure not only my survival, but Catherine's, Georgina's and Heidi's. I lit a cigarette and checked my watch: 9.45pm. Fifteen minutes to go before the agreed time to meet Sir David.

A voice behind me made me turn round.

"Michael McLoughlan?"

The man walking towards me was not David Gough. He was about the same age, mid fifties, tall, and smartly dressed.

"My name is Astor, Peter Astor. Sir David has asked me to collect some papers we understand have come into your possession."

"I have some papers, that's correct – not on me but not far away. However, I don't intend releasing them to anyone without first speaking to Sir David."

"That I'm afraid is completely out of the question. Sir David is out of the country until next week. So if these papers are, as we are led to believe, important, then I must insist you make them available immediately. Alternatively, I'll have one of my officers arrest you."

"That sounds interesting Mr Astor, but if that happens, copies of what I hold will be with every newspaper and media organisation in the world within forty-eight hours."

"You're not really attempting to make some sort of deal are you, Mr McLoughlan? Not against Her Majesty's secret service surely?"

"That's exactly what I'm doing, Mr Astor, not just with our government but perhaps more towards Sir David Gough and his interests in British and American Oil Refineries. But to be quite frank I don't much care what title you give yourselves. I'm telling you, I'm ready to do a very simple deal with your boss or the shit hits the fan, so to speak. So make up your mind."

That was it – I'd fired all my guns. There was no point in delaying things. Either my plan was going to work or it wasn't. I was about to find out.

"You remind me very much of myself, Mr McLoughlan, twenty years or so ago."

The voice came from the figure of a man walking towards me as he emerged from the shadows. I recognised him. It was Sir David Gough. Smiling, he held out his hand which I shook.

"You're a very confident young man, Mr McLoughlan. I think it's perhaps time we had a chat, don't you?"

"Sir David, you're welcome to all the papers I've been given on the condition that nothing happens to me, Georgina, Catherine McKenzie or Heidi Gantevoort for the next fifty years or so. Should anything untoward happen to any one of us I have given explicit instructions for copies of all the documents you're so anxious to retrieve to be forwarded to every newspaper and media organisation in the world."

"Looks like you've got us by the balls, Michael. It's a deal then. Hand the papers over and that'll be the end of it."

There was nothing to gain by prolonging things, I thought. My only guarantee was the fact I held the copies – copies which, if any media organisation got hold of, would cause unimaginable problems, not only for our security services but for the government as well. However, there was one other part of the deal I needed to secure.

"In addition to the guarantee of our safety, Sir David, you will arrange a payment in the sum of £1 million for the credit of my private account, to be received within the next forty-eight hours."

Sir David looked at me and smiled.

"You almost disappointed me for a moment. I was beginning to think you'd forgotten all about your fees. Give Peter your bank details and I'll have the transfer made immediately."

I took out the A4 envelope and handed it over.

"I imagine your surveillance officers already have my account details, Sir David. They're in the letter I posted in the mailbox over the road a few moments ago. I think you'll find they've managed to retrieve it by now."

He laughed.

"It's a pity we won't be meeting again. I know I could do business with you. Good luck to you, and your business."

I watched as Peter Astor and Sir David Gough walked briskly down the Thames footpath, closely followed by several of their security officers.

I felt completely drained. I got a taxi to the station and caught the train back home to Birchwood House Farm. Maybe now, I thought, I'd get a chance to have a proper look around the place.

Chapter 36

I arrived back at Birchwood House Farm just after 2.30am. There was a note on the hall table from Theresa, informing me Carol had telephoned to say she'd be back tomorrow. Her sister Angela had given birth to a baby boy, 6lbs 4oz. Both mother and baby were doing fine. There were also three A4 pages of messages concerning MCL Carriers, which I thought could wait till morning. I went upstairs, climbed into bed and slept like a log.

I woke at 7am, showered, dressed, went downstairs and made myself some toast. I took this, together with a mug of coffee and my cigarettes, out onto the patio. I sat down at the wrought iron table and chairs overlooking the gardens. After this relaxed start to the day, I walked over to the garage and checked over a few things with Gordon, who told me he was pleased with his new assistant but that we needed a new pit and hydraulic ramp to keep up with the extra work. With the increase in mileage our trucks were doing, not to mention the additional trucks he'd be servicing from August onwards, they'd need to be able to work on more than one vehicle at a time. I'd already planned for this and told Gordon we'd get the extra ramp and pit sorted out next month.

I went over to the office. Theresa and her new assistants had arrived. The phone was busy, and two new customers had made contact with us – the orders were increasing. Theresa was doing a great job and so obviously enjoying the challenge. I went through the paperwork on my desk, checked over the costing for two new enquiries and signed some cheques. Then a phone call came through for me: Martin Evans, my business manager at Barclays Bank.

"Michael, good morning. I thought I'd let you know we have just received a rather large transfer into your current account for £1 million."

"I was expecting that. Not all for me but there's a decent profit there. Can you transfer £250,000 into the savings account? I have plans for the remainder and will be making some payments over the next few days."

"Not a problem, Michael. I'll arrange that straight away for you. I would be delighted to call round to see you when you have a moment, see how you're settling into your new premises."

I said I'd call him in the next couple of weeks and arrange a meeting here at Birchwood House Farm. Switching on my computer, I went into the Hotmail account to check if the 'hush hush' message received from Catherine last week was still in the inbox. If it was, I could send a reply informing her of what looked like a successful conclusion to the meeting with Sir David Gough. Catherine's message had been deleted, but there was a new message from her. I went through the same question and answer routine as before and then the message appeared.

Michael,
Helen Mason's address, as requested:
Mrs Helen Mason
34 Greenwood Avenue
Stratford-upon-Avon
CV37 5HF
Catherine

I touched the reply button.

Catherine,
Deal accepted. Safe to contact Georgina. Check your account
later. Get Georgina the treatment she needs. Then get that
cottage in St Ives.
Michael

I wrote out a cheque for £250,000 payable to Helen Mason and handwrote a short note which I hoped sounded plausible.

Dear Helen,
I read with sadness the news of your husband's untimely
demise in Paris. I have just won a rather large amount of
money on the lottery and hope you'll accept the enclosed.
Yours truly,
A well-wisher

I went into the lounge and telephoned Heidi. She answered almost immediately.

"Heidi, it's Michael. How are you?"

"Feeling a little better after our meeting, Michael, and getting rid of all that poison I gave you."

"I'm glad you're feeling better. I have some news which should make you feel better still. The problems we had, I believe they have now been resolved. I can't go into things too much you understand, but you can start now to move on, so to speak. Get that career in teaching underway. Heidi, I've got something which will give you some practical help. Give me your bank details."

"What on earth for? What's this all about?"

"Just let me have your bank details and stop asking questions."

Heidi gave me the details.

"Just check your account next week, then start making plans

for yourself. And good luck with everything."

I put down the receiver, went back to the office and made two transfers: one to Catherine McKenzie for £250,000 and one to Heidi Gantevoort for £250,000. One more cheque, I thought: a bonus for Theresa. I wrote a cheque for £10,000 and put it in an envelope with a note.

Theresa,
I couldn't manage without you.
Michael

It had crossed my mind to keep the £1 million. It would not only have paid off my mortgage and all the loans but left a sizeable sum. But I knew I'd made the right decision, for me anyway. Operation Aries had almost destroyed Catherine who'd discovered the decision made by MI6 to eliminate her. Georgina could now get the very best treatment for her cancer. Heidi had lost her boyfriend, shot by some faceless thug, and Helen Mason had lost her husband and father of their two children simply because he'd booked into the wrong room at the Hotel Campanile. All I'd had to deal with was to duck the odd couple of bullets and lose one of my trucks. And according to the letter received this morning from our insurer, a payment to cover most of the loss would be forwarded in the next few days.

I picked up the phone and called Carol.

"I've been back about an hour, Michael. How are you? And what have you been up to? Theresa said you've been over to Paris for some more business deals. How did they go?"

"Not bad, Carol. In fact we can afford a holiday now, and I've decided I'm giving the decorating a miss. I'll get Barry and his team to finish it all. So, a bit more time for us now. How do you fancy a holiday?"

"Sounds absolutely brilliant – where are you going to whisk me away to? South of France, Venice?"

"To be honest, Carol, I've seen enough of Europe for the moment."

There was a pause.

"Bournemouth then?"

"Good idea, Carol, and the weather forecast is good for a change."

Carol laughed.

"You're certainly one for the simple life, Michael."

Simple life? I thought.

How I wish.

Lightning Source UK Ltd.
Milton Keynes UK
UKOW051958280613

212929UK00002B/54/P